Quinn blinked. Why was he cataloging her looks like that? He cleared his throat sharply, bringing her attention snapping in his direction. "Uh…did we have a meeting I forgot about?"

"No," she answered. She didn't elaborate, looking away again. Everything in her body language screamed she didn't want to be here, but…here she was. In his pro shop. Where she'd been maybe four times since he'd started working here.

"Is there something I can help you with?"

She hesitated, then looked his way again. "You do lessons, right?"

"*Golf* lessons? Well, it's my job, so…yeah." Had someone complained about a class? "Is there a problem I need to know about?"

"No, sorry." She finally walked over to the counter to face him. "I'm not sure why I'm doing this, but…do you think you could give me lessons?"

"*Golf* lessons?" He blurted the words out again. Julie had never expressed any interest in, or respect for, the game of golf.

"Unless there's something else you teach, yes, I'd like golf lessons."

"Why?" He thought of their meeting a few days earlier. "Was this Blake's idea? Because I can talk to him and—"

"Is the thought of giving me a couple golf lessons that terrible?"

Dear Reader,

When I'm writing a series, certain characters tend to hover in the background of other stories for a while until it's their turn to shine. In this case, it's Julie Brown, manager of the Gallant Lake Resort and Spa. She's been a good friend in several books, but she's getting tired of always being a bridesmaid in someone else's wedding. When will it be *her* turn?

Her coworker, golf pro Quinn Walker, is in the opposite situation. Still grieving the death of his wife and busy raising a teenage daughter, he wants *nothing* to do with dating. But when Julie reluctantly starts taking golf lessons from him, their territorial skirmishes between the resort and the golf course provide a surprising spark for a love neither expected.

I've been promising my husband and our golfing friends a golf romance, and this is it! While I love a cowboy or a billionaire as much as the next reader, I enjoy introducing heroes from different walks of life in my books. I see the potential sexiness in hardware-store owners (*Changing His Plans*) and golfers like Quinn.

Gallant Lake is a town where friendships run deep. Julie's friends there have become her found family, since her real family was...less than great. In this story, those friends know when she needs a little encouragement, a shoulder to cry on, a few laughs or a dose of "oh, honey, no."

I couldn't have written this book without the encouragement of my own wonderful friends. Or without the love of my real-life hero, Himself. And, of course, the support of my wonderful agent, Veronica Park of Fuse Literary.

Happy reading!

Jo

Second-Chance Summer

JO McNALLY

HARLEQUIN

SPECIAL
EDITION

HARLEQUIN
SPECIAL EDITION™

Recycling programs
for this product may
not exist in your area.

ISBN-13: 978-1-335-40853-2

Second-Chance Summer

Copyright © 2022 by Jo McNally

Harlequin Enterprises ULC
22 Adelaide St. West, 41st Floor
Toronto, Ontario M5H 4E3, Canada
www.Harlequin.com

Printed in U.S.A.

Jo McNally lives in upstate New York with one hundred pounds of dog and two hundred pounds of husband—her slice of the bed is very small. When she's not writing or reading romance novels (or clinging to the edge of the bed), she can often be found on the back porch sipping wine with friends while listening to great music. If the weather is absolutely perfect, Jo might join her husband on the golf course, where she tends to feel far more competitive than her actual skill level would suggest.

You can follow Jo pretty much anywhere on social media—and she'd love it if you did—but you can start at her website, jomcnallyromance.com.

Books by Jo McNally

Harlequin Special Edition

Gallant Lake Stories

A Man You Can Trust
It Started at Christmas...
Her Homecoming Wish
Changing His Plans
Her Mountainside Haven

The Fortunes of Texas: The Wedding Gift

A Soldier's Dare

HQN

Rendezvous Falls

Slow Dancing at Sunrise
Stealing Kisses in the Snow
Sweet Nothings by Moonlight
Barefoot on a Starlit Night
Love Blooms
When Sparks Fly

Visit the Author Profile page
at Harlequin.com for more titles.

This book is dedicated to a friend who
has believed in me from the moment I said,
"Hey, I'm going to write a romance!" She's always
known when I needed a laugh, a shoulder to
cry on, an adventure or a strong dose of reality.

To Liz with love and thanks.

Chapter One

"You can't *possibly* have a closet just for your—"

Julie Brown yanked open the closet door in her spare room, then turned to face her best friend, Amanda Randall, hand on her hip. "You were saying?"

"Holy…" Amanda stepped forward, running her hand along the hangers that held nothing but bridesmaid dresses. "I don't know if I should be impressed or horrified. I had no idea you'd been a bridesmaid so many…" She started to laugh, then caught herself, covering her mouth. "I'm sorry, but all I can think of is that movie—"

"*27 Dresses*? Yeah, I know." Julie sighed. "But in

the movie, the character did it because she loved weddings so much."

They stared at the colorful array of gowns and cocktail dresses. Satin. Polyester. Velvet. Cotton. Pink. Black. Orange. Blue. Her wide range of friends and family represented an equally wide range of fashion tastes, and Julie had gone along with them all. It was funny at first, the whole always-a-bridesmaid-and-never-a-bride schtick. But this last wedding—a high school classmate's *third* in the twenty-two years since graduation—had been the one that made her confront that proverbial clock ticking away on her life.

"But you love weddings, too, right?" Amanda reached in and pulled out an elegant gown of deep pink silk. "And you weren't always a bridesmaid. You were *my* maid of honor in this dress and you looked gorgeous." Amanda held out the dress and frowned at it. "You should shorten this into a cocktail dress. I'll bet you could find an occasion to wear it. It's full of happy memories, right?"

"You know I love you, and your Christmas wedding in your Christmas castle was a magical day. But it was *your* day." Julie took the dress from Amanda and squinted at it. "The saving grace for this one is that it was custom-designed by your cousin, Mel, so at least it has some style. But how often do you see me wearing pink?" Melanie Brannigan was a former model turned designer turned small-town boutique owner. Her shop in Gallant Lake—Five and Design—was one of Julie's favorite places, but more for sweaters and jeans than couture gowns.

"It definitely has more style than some of these others." Amanda pulled out a peacock-blue sequined short dress with a floor-length train of teal tulle. "This is, uh, a statement?"

Julie let out a groan. "My cousin's idea of a classy wedding theme. The train was supposed to be our 'tail.' We each had a peacock feather in our hair. This fabric is like chainmail. By the end of the reception I was ready to squawk like a peacock and fly away."

They both laughed, and Julie felt her tension easing. Amanda always found a way to get her smiling, even in the middle of a mini midlife crisis. Amanda started counting when she put back the sparkly dress.

"You don't quite have twenty-seven."

"Thank God for small favors. There are fourteen dresses here. I'm telling you right now, there won't be a fifteenth, no matter *who* asks me. I'm done." She closed the door and they went back to her kitchen.

The house was small and tidy, just the way Julie liked things. Located on one of Gallant Lake's quiet side streets, the cute 1950s ranch was close to her job at the Gallant Lake Resort and Spa, which was

owned by Amanda and her husband, Blake. It was
also close enough to Main Street that Julie could
walk there, which she often did, taking the newly
expanded lakeshore trail through a small park and
into town. The trail would take her all the way to
the resort if she cut through the golf course, but
she preferred to show up to work without being
out of breath from a long uphill hike. And the golfers got really huffy if they found anyone walking
along their cart paths. That stuck-up golf pro, Quinn
Walker, got even huffier.

Amanda sat at the vintage red Formica-topped
kitchen table and took a cookie from the plate in
front of her. There were three different recipes represented there. Julie often cooked on Mondays—
her day off—for stress relief, and this last weekend
had built up some *major* stress to be relieved. There
were two big weddings at the resort with guests
flying in from all over the country. They'd hired
multiple shuttle vans and limos, but the logistics of
dealing with pickups and drop-offs at JFK, LaGuar-
dia and Newark with multiple flight delays due to
spring storms in the southeast had just about broken
Julie and her team. When one bride's grandmother
arrived at JFK only two hours before the wedding
ceremony, it was Julie herself who had driven to the
city to make sure Grandma made it.

Amanda closed her eyes and moaned with pleasure. She often stopped by to help Julie dispense with her cooking projects.

"Oh. My. God. What *is* this?"

"It's a German crescent cookie. The dough is actually yeast-based, with sour cream in it. A bit of a pain to make, but I think it was worth it, don't you?"

"Oh, hell yeah. This is amazing. Can I take some home to Blake and the kids?"

"Of course. I have almost five dozen of the things." Julie took a crescent for herself. They really were yummy. "I found an old German cookbook at the flea market last week and I'm going to work my way through it in honor of Grandma Ina."

She refilled their coffee mugs and sat at the table. The nearby window overlooked a yard as simple and tidy as the house.

"You know, I keep thinking about your bridesmaid closet," Amanda said. "Some of those dresses could be salvaged into something more practical. You should talk to Mel." She winked. "Except the peacock dress. That needs to go."

"Trust me, that's not the only dress that has to go." Julie set down her coffee. "And where exactly do you think I'm going to wear the others?"

"You manage the swankiest resort in the Catskills, my dear. There are plenty of events you could dress up for."

"I *work* most of those events, my *dear*. I'd think my boss would remember that."

Amanda's nose wrinkled. "Ew. Don't call me that. Blake, maybe, but you and I are friends first. Besides, you *run* the place, so you can wear what you want."

"You know how much running around I do. Practicality first for me." Julie always laughed when people complained about how hard it was to get in 10,000 steps a day. That was a *slow* day for her. The three-story historic lakefront resort had over two hundred rooms, two ballrooms, a restaurant, spa, a pool and, of course, the golf course. As if reading her mind, Amanda finished her coffee and waggled her eyebrows at Julie.

"Our big charity golf tournament is coming up in August. Blake said we're booked to the rafters. There's bound to be someplace to wear a pretty dress there."

"For what purpose? Just to dust them off and bring them out of my closet?"

"Think about it—you said you don't always want to be a bridesmaid. Well, maybe it's time to get more proactive in finding a potential groom. Lots of well-heeled men at the tournament."

Julie rolled her eyes. "I'm not looking for a sugar daddy. I want to meet a nice guy to share my life with before I turn into some spinster cat lady." Right on cue, her calico cat, Fluff, walked into the kitchen, paused to give the women a baleful stare, then sauntered into the living room. Julie leveled a stern look at Amanda. "And that golf tournament isn't exactly my favorite weekend anymore. Not since Walker showed up."

In the three years that he'd been in charge of the golf course at the resort, Walker and she had butted heads more than once. Blake Randall called them *territorial skirmishes*, since Quinn ran the course and Julie managed the resort itself. They always seemed to have lots of opinions on how the other ran their end of things.

The Travis Foundation Charity Weekend was the biggest annual event the resort held. It benefited a charity Amanda's North Carolina cousin, Bree Caldwell, had established to help veterans adapt to civilian life, particularly those with PTSD or physical injuries. Bree was a former Hollywood reality television star, so the event often drew a few celebrities along with other affluent golfers. The stakes were high, and so were tempers when Julie and Quinn worked on the schedule and logistics of it all.

"I don't get it." Amanda flipped her long blond curls over her shoulder and grabbed another crescent cookie. "You and Quinn are two of the nicest people I know, and you can't stand each other."

"He said he can't stand me?" Julie straightened, trying to ignore the pinprick she felt against her pride.

"Of course not. It's just the impression I get from both of you. Whenever you work together, you end up arguing. And he really is a nice man. I mean, he quit the pro tour to raise his daughter after his wife died, and—"

"I know, I know." Julie waved her hand to stop Amanda from reciting his impressive biography. "And I do respect what he did for Katie. She's a lovely young woman. In fact, she's going to intern at the resort this summer before she heads off to college. But Quinn is so, I don't know…pretentious? He acts like *golf* is a real sport and takes it all so seriously." Julie was more of a football and hockey fan herself.

"Well, it *is* his livelihood—"

"Yes, but good grief. It's a country club, not a cathedral. All those rules and whispered voices and ridiculous plaid shorts. I stopped by once on my day off to drop off some brochures, and I was in denim shorts. Everyone stared at me like I was Lady Godiva riding in there naked. *Especially* Quinn. He scolded me about it like I was some heathen come to destroy their sanctuary. I told him to get a grip, which made some of the guys snicker for some reason…" She paused, noting Amanda's curiously unreadable expression. "What?"

"Nothing!" Amanda folded her napkin carefully, her mouth pinched as if she was holding in laughter. "I didn't realize you'd leased the man quite so much space in your head, that's all."

"I know you think he's a saint, but you don't

know him like I do. That Mr. Nice Guy routine isn't genuine, at least not on the job. He doesn't listen, and I swear he looks down his nose at me. Thank God we only have to work together on the big events and can ignore each other the rest of the time."

"Again…" Amanda moved her hand in a circular motion, gesturing at Julie. "*Lots* of headspace."

"That woman is going to be the death of me." Quinn Walker stared at his computer screen in disbelief. "I seriously think she's trying to kill me by giving me a heart attack."

His eighteen-year-old daughter looked up from the nest she'd built in what used to be Quinn's recliner. Katie's strawberry blond hair fell across her face, like Anne's used to do. Even worse, she reached up with one finger and flipped it back over her shoulder, exactly like Anne would have. Four years later, it still pinched his heart.

Katie had taken over Quinn's chair a year ago and *enhanced* it with pillows, a furry pink throw and a pastel quilt that had belonged to her mother. She was curled up in the seat, tablet in hand, feet tucked under herself. He'd get his chair back when she went off to college in August. It was a thought that brought him no joy.

She plucked out one earbud and shook her head at him. "Let me take a wild guess. Julie Brown did something to tick you off again. Like…breathing. Existing on the planet."

"Yeah, yeah, everyone loves Saint Julie." His temper cooled somewhat as he acknowledged that the resort manager had always been kind to Katie and had even offered her a paid internship that summer. "But she's not like that with me. She's a constant thorn in my side, and I think she *wants* to be the thorn. Every time we agree on a schedule for the Travis Foundation weekend, she goes and changes it without telling me." He gestured toward his laptop.

"She has the practice round teeing off at one o'clock on Friday when I told her we should tee off at eleven. And she has some fancy cocktail-hour thing starting at the resort at *five*. If we don't tee off until one, the teams won't even be off the course by five, much less showered, changed and ready for cocktails." He shoved the laptop in frustration, trying not to show his concern when it came perilously close to the edge of the kitchen island where he was sitting. "Besides, Friday is the fun night for the golf teams. It's when we announce the team flights and golfers figure out the best teams to sponsor." That was a nice way of saying which teams to bet on. "It's *our* night."

"You sound like a pouty five-year-old stomping your feet about getting your way. You two have this battle every year, Dad. Figure it out already."

If only it was that easy. He and Julie Brown did

not see eye-to-eye. They weren't sworn enemies or anything—it wasn't as if they'd ever had some big, unforgivable battle over anything. But she had a habit of changing things without telling him and generally making his life as the golf pro for Gallant Lake Golf Club more difficult.

He fired off an email in response to her schedule change and told her the revised schedule would not work for the golfers. He reminded her that this was, first and foremost, a *golf* tournament. It was his job to keep the golfers happy. It was Julie's job to keep the spouses and partners happy while the golfers golfed. Spa treatments. Shopping excursions through the Catskills. That was her domain. The golf course was his.

Of course, the actual email didn't contain that exact wording, but he was sure she'd get the message. A one-o'clock tee time wasn't happening. Neither was a five-o'clock cocktail party. Nice try. *Thank you, next.* Before he hit Send, he included an offer to schedule a meeting—perhaps with Blake Randall in attendance—to hammer out a schedule for the big weekend that would work for *both* of them.

Invoking Blake's name wasn't an automatic win for Quinn. He got along great with his boss, who'd renewed his love of golf since Quinn's arrival three years ago. The two of them often played a few holes in the late evening, when things were quiet. He'd like to think they'd become friends. Blake seemed happy with the golf course operations.

But Julie had been maid of honor at Blake and Amanda's wedding at the historic stone mansion they called home. When it came to scoring points with the boss, she probably held the upper hand. And she wouldn't hesitate to use that advantage against him.

Her email response came fast and hot.

Fine. I'll set up a meeting. Tomorrow afternoon work for you?

He grinned as he read it. He'd ticked her off, for sure. He could play the cool one, too. He sent his response.

Sounds good.

He was looking forward to seeing her. *No, wait...* He was looking forward to convincing her he was right about the tee times. There was no reason in the world he'd look forward to just...seeing her. It was something he actively avoided.

Chapter Two

Julie stood in the small staff room behind the front desk and frowned at the schedule on the wall. They had three wedding receptions that coming weekend, and one of them had more than two hundred guests. The resort would be packed. The staffing schedule, however, was *not* packed. The new computerized scheduling software Blake had purchased was not working as advertised. Instead of making her job easier, it was causing new headaches she didn't need. She'd have to make some calls and convince a few people to work on their weekend off.

"Is that whiteboard fascinating in some way I'm not seeing?" Cassie West stepped up next to Julie.

Cassie was the vice president of operations for Randall Resorts International and worked in the second-floor corporate offices. The Gallant Lake Resort itself was one of Blake Randall's smaller hotel properties. He owned five others in more exotic locales, like Miami, San Francisco and Bali.

Julie sighed and shook her head. "I'm just calculating how much staff we're going to need this weekend and—" she gestured at the board "—this isn't going to work."

"Computer system again?" Julie nodded and Cassie patted her shoulder. "Blake is furious about all the glitches, but the vendor's tech team is coming next week to try to straighten it out. Blake made Nick the point person, since it was his idea to try it in the first place." Cassie giggled about her husband being on the hot seat over this. "The company is blaming the data input—"

"There was nothing wrong with my data," Julie growled. She pointed at the board. "And there was nothing wrong with my system."

"Don't worry. Nick told them to figure it out or else, and you know how intimidating he can be!"

Cassie had met her now-husband, Nick West, here at the resort. She'd been an executive assistant to both Blake and Nick, the head of security for all of the resorts.

"Speaking of schedules—" Cassie nudged Julie's shoulder "—I saw Blake has a meeting on his calendar this afternoon with you and your nemesis. What did Quinn do this time?"

Among her many duties, Cassie helped Blake and Nick stay organized. Julie turned away from the schedule and poured herself a cup of coffee from the commercial machine in the corner. She offered Cassie a cup, but the new mom reached past her and grabbed the orange-topped decaf pot.

"No real coffee for me until Emily is done nursing. Now spill on the Quinn situation."

Julie worried her lip for a moment, knowing that Nick and Cassie were good friends with Quinn and his daughter, Katie. But this wasn't personal. It was business, and Cassie was as good about maintaining those boundaries as Julie was.

"Apparently he's having a fit about the schedule I created for the big benefit weekend in August. All he thinks about is his precious golf course, but he's really just one part of the event."

Cassie sipped her coffee, her eyebrows arching high. "Um…isn't the golf tournament the whole point of the weekend? I mean, that's how it all started, right?"

"Well…yeah. But then we added the fashion show and the day trips for the nongolfers, so he needs to—" She caught herself and softened the statement. "*We* need to work as a team. And that man is not a team player."

Cassie shook her head, clearly unconvinced. "I

gotta be honest, Jules. I've never known Quinn to be self-centered or unreasonable."

"Yeah, I know. Quinn is a saint among men and everyone loves him. But it's different between him and me. It feels so adversarial."

"*Feels* or *is*? I love you, girl, but it takes two to do battle."

Julie thought about that for a minute—the possibility of her being part of the problem—then dismissed it.

"He's such a typical *man*. He announces what he wants and expects everyone to just go along." Her eyes narrowed on Cassie. "And you all worship his widower, single-dad schtick, so he gets his way. Except with me."

"Whoa. What *is* it about him that bugs you so much? I know your dad was a jerk, but…" Cassie's eyes went wide. "Oh, my God, are you mad at Quinn because he's giving Katie everything your dad didn't give you?"

"What? No. Please don't psychoanalyze me, Cass. I know you're into all that psychology stuff, but it's not for me. My dad *was* awful. So was my mom. But I'm fine." She gestured down to herself. "Look at me—I've got my degree, I'm working on my MBA, I run the nicest resort in the Catskills. I don't have daddy issues and my childhood didn't slow me down one bit." Julie prided herself on her success. And she was sure she'd be successful in convincing her boss that her plan worked better than Quinn's.

A few hours later in Blake Randall's office, she was trying to remind her very professional, determined self that she would *not* throw her planning folder for the benefit weekend at Quinn Walker's head.

They were sitting side by side across from Blake. The massive oak desk, with its irregular-shaped, gleaming surface made from a slab of a huge oak tree felled in a storm, made the meeting more formal than usual. Blake usually had staff members sit with him at the small round table by the far window overlooking the resort's expansive lawn that led down to the lakeshore. He'd serve coffee, maybe have a platter of cookies on hand, sit back in one of the soft leather armchairs and tell funny stories about something that happened at another of his resorts to break the ice. None of that happened today. He was very much in boss mode.

Blake was tall and broad-shouldered, with black wavy hair and chiseled features. There was a time when he'd scared the daylights out of Julie with his scowling demeanor and the way he'd barked out orders around the resort. Then he'd fallen in love with Amanda and she'd found a way to soften him around the edges. As Julie and Amanda had grown close as friends, he'd assured Julie that the personal relationship would never affect his business decisions about the resort. Heck, she had dinner at the historic castle he and Amanda called home at least once or twice a month. But you'd never know it from his expression right now. He fixed his stern, dark eyes on her.

"I'm confused. Haven't you two already done two of these benefit weekends together? Why is there suddenly an issue with the schedule—" he glanced Quinn's way, showing his irritation was split equally "—that you two can't figure out without involving me? Do you really think the best use of my time is negotiating when the cocktail hour will start?"

"Of course not," Julie said quickly. "I've already said the Friday night cocktail hour will be at five."

Quinn cleared his throat next to her, obviously feeling the same coolness from Blake that she was. He was dressed in his usual golf attire, with solid blue shorts and a blue-and-green striped shirt. He might be irritating, but he was also undeniably good-looking. His light brown hair looked as if he'd pulled off a golf cap right before the meeting and run his fingers through it, making it stand up in curling waves. He was tall and lean with powerful shoulders. His skin was tanned and weathered from years golfing in the sun. She forgot her silent admiration when his chocolate eyes narrowed. "The only way that will work is if the Friday tee times start at eleven, and even then it's going to be tight."

Blake threw his hands up in frustration. "Then set the tee time at eleven."

Quinn pointed at her. "*She* has them starting at one."

If you don't take that pointy finger away from my face...

He lowered his hand, mumbling an apology. Oh, God, had she said that out loud? No, he probably just read her face.

Blake turned to her. "Why is the resort setting tee times at the golf course? That's not your—"

"I just thought we'd try a nice brunch on Friday. One that includes the golfers and their guests together. We could have a carving station with prime rib and ham, and we'll serve mimosas…" Her voice trailed off at the two incredulous faces looking at her right now. "What? You told me you wanted us to change things up each year so it's never stale, and this would…do that?" That roaring determination of hers was fading fast.

Quinn looked at Blake, and their amused she's-so-clueless expressions sparked her temper. She sat up straight, her voice turning sharp. "Let me in on the joke, boys. Why is that such a bad idea?"

Blake started to answer, but Quinn talked over him. "Not bad. And not a joke. I'm sorry if it felt that way." Of course, he was going to be *nice* in front of Blake. "It's just that we get some serious players for this tournament, ones with deep pockets.

We need to prioritize the golf portion of the weekend for them." He was still being nice, with a warm smile and softer voice. She wasn't used to it, and a strange sensation crept up her spine as he continued. "No serious golfer wants to play right after a full meal. They also don't want to be teeing off in the heat of the day, knowing they'll never be finished in time to shower and change for some cocktail party their spouses will insist they attend at five o'clock. That doesn't make for relaxed golfing."

She wanted to argue. She'd always thought golfers were way too serious about their so-called sport. But Quinn was right about the deep pockets. And the point of the weekend was to raise as much money as possible for the veterans' charity. Julie's older brother, Bobby, was a veteran. He was one of the lucky ones who came home whole, both physically and emotionally, but some of his buddies hadn't been as fortunate. Julie leaned back in her chair, knowing she'd lost this round. Maybe Cassie had a point about her clinging to her own stubbornness.

"Okay. Maybe I developed some tunnel vision here. I was excited about having a nice cocktail party on the veranda of the resort." She shrugged. "I guess I'll have to come up with something else."

Quinn rested his elbows on his knees. The weathered creases at the edges of his eyes deepened with his smile.

"Golfers can have tunnel vision, too. Present company included." He put one hand on his chest. "It's not that they want to avoid their spouses all weekend, but they are going to be focused on the game. They're spending big bucks to play, and the purse is substantial. Maybe we can come up with a compromise?"

Blake studied something on his computer screen, then started typing. "If you can do that in the next ten minutes, that'd be awesome."

Julie shrugged. "I'm listening."

"What if, instead of a brunch with lunch items, we did a fancier breakfast for everyone?" Quinn warmed up to the idea as he spoke, his eyes brightening. "Waffles and made-to-order omelets. If we had that at nine, the golfers could be on the course comfortably by eleven. And their guests would be free to do an excursion in the afternoon. Maybe plan something special?"

Blake whistled a melody to himself softly, clearly pleased with the suggestion.

She thought for a moment. "That could work. I've been thinking of adding a bus ride up to Walkway Over the Hudson State Park, and that's an hour away." The former railroad trestle was now a pedestrian walkway more than a mile long, high above the Hudson River. "What about the cocktail party?"

Blake's song stopped, and he whistled the equivalent of *uh-oh.*

Quinn frowned. He clearly wasn't enthusiastic about the idea of a cocktail party. Then he sat up with a smile, snapping his fingers.

"We'll do it at the clubhouse!"

"Do *what*? The cocktail party? The kitchen is too small there."

"Prepare the food at the resort and bring it to the club," Quinn answered. "It would be more casual, but would give the golfers a chance to bring their guests into their world, instead of dashing to the resort all the time."

Blake started whistling happily again.

Her eyes narrowed. "And what's wrong with the resort?"

The whistling stopped abruptly. Blake gave her an exasperated look. "Seriously? That's all you got from Quinn's suggestion?"

She pressed her lips together so tightly she'd be surprised if there was any color in them at all. She was making a mess of this. Quinn was coming out as the magnanimous coworker so very eager to co-operate, while she was acting like a spoiled brat.

"I'm sorry." She barely heard her own words. She cleared her throat. "That idea could work, I guess. Casual. We could have fun with that."

Blake nodded. "We already have the black-tie banquet on Saturday night. Maybe we give Friday night a more fun theme."

"Theme? Ooh, that would be fun…"

Quinn groaned. "We're not having a pirate night at the golf course."

"Maybe not pirates. But…"

He rolled his eyes. "Why can't it be a relaxing little get-together? Beer, wine, finger food. The golfers would be fresh off the course. Isn't that theme enough?"

"Agreed." Blake made the one word sound like a final verdict, and Julie knew it was a done deal. He looked between her and Quinn. "Anything else you need me to mediate between you two?"

"No," she and Quinn responded in unison.

Blake stared hard at them, then leaned back in his chair with a low chuckle. "So I can put away my stern-brunch-daddy face and talk to you two like friends?"

Julie was so surprised she couldn't help bursting into laughter.

"Did you just call yourself a *stern brunch daddy* in a business meeting?" She wiped tears from the corner of her eyes.

Blake's cheeks went a tinge darker. "Why? It means being serious, right? Using my serious parenting face. Amanda calls me that…" His eyes fell closed. "Oh, God, what does it *really* mean?"

"It's a romance-novel term, Blake. It means a guy who might be sophisticated or reserved in public, but when he gets behind the bedroom doors, he's…" She suddenly remembered that it wasn't just her and Blake sitting at his dinner table with her best friend, Amanda. They were in his office and they weren't alone. Quinn raised one eyebrow, waiting for her to continue.

Blake was laughing now, too. "Behind the bedroom doors…what? At least tell me it's a compliment."

"Uh…" Now it was her turn to blush. "Yes. Hence the, uh, *stern* part. In, um…" How had she gotten into this conversation? "In control, if you know what I mean." She waved her hand back and forth in an attempt to erase the conversation. "Anyway, my point is that you may not want to refer to yourself that way at work."

Quinn snorted, trying to hold in a laugh. What was even happening with this conversation right now? It had gone relatively well from his perspective, with Blake agreeing that Quinn should be the one to set the golf schedules. She wasn't happy about it, but she'd finally conceded to a few compromises. It was a win for him. And then, just like that, the conversation veered into some unintended sexual innuendo on Blake's part. No way did Quinn want to wade into any potentially suggestive conversations with Julie Brown. In their boss's office or anywhere else.

But her laughter did something to him. He'd seen her laughing with her friends before, but never had he been this close to her. Her dark eyes lit up, and the laugh lines near her eyes deepened, slanting upward like the smile on her lips. Quinn felt as if something was knotting up inside of him. Or more accurately…*un*knotting. Breaking loose. Breaking free. He cocked an eyebrow at her and before he could censor himself, he blurted out a question that was guaranteed to lead to trouble.

"And what romance-novel term would you use for me?"

Her laughter stopped abruptly. For someone who didn't want to wade into this conversation, he'd managed to do a cannonball into the pool. Blake was still chuckling, probably secretly preening over his wife calling him such a provocative term.

"My best guess is cinnamon roll." Julie gave him a once-over with her gaze.

Blake roared with laughter, but Quinn stiffened. "Cinnamon roll? What the hell does *that* mean?" *Stern brunch daddy* sounded a hell of a lot sexier than *cinnamon roll*. Not that he cared if Julie found him sexy or not, but still. *Cinnamon roll?*

Julie dropped her head back and stared at the ceiling before closing her eyes tightly. "Why are we talking about this? And why did I answer either of you?" She stood abruptly, nearly dropping the folder that had been in her lap. She always had a folder or binder of some sort. He'd heard her tell someone that she was old-school when it came to planning. She liked something tactile, like paper and binders and whiteboards with different color markers. Once she'd secured the folder, she looked between the two men. "You are such children." She glanced at Quinn. "A cinnamon-roll hero is sweet. Maybe crusty on the outside, but soft and warm on the inside. Some people say they're too good to be true. A unicorn. Something that doesn't exist in real life."

With that, she walked out of the office, leaving both Quinn and Blake gaping at the open door. Blake shook his head with a slow smile.

"She's so quietly brilliant at what she does here that I sometimes forget how kick-ass she can be. I used to think she was too mousy to be manager, and then I found out she'd gone behind my back to make policy changes and marketing decisions that helped this place survive after the casino plans fell through."

Quinn knew the story. Blake originally bought the resort and the neglected castle next door with plans to raze everything and build a large casino in Gallant Lake. The only problem was that Gallant Lake residents didn't *want* a casino. They organized and took him to court, claiming the mansion, named Halcyon, was a historic landmark and couldn't be torn down. And they'd won.

"How long has Julie worked for you?"

"From the moment I bought the place. She's been at the resort longer than I have—she worked for the former owners and kept the place stumbling along when they started to struggle financially. Speaking of unicorns, she *is* one—she started in Housekeeping straight out of high school and worked her way up from there. She doesn't take anything for granted, either. She earned her bachelor's online, and now she's working on her MBA." He gave Quinn a hard look. "And most people here adore her. What is it with you two?"

He scrubbed his hands over his face. "I honestly don't know. We're not competitors, but it always feels like we're competing, anyway. She's so freakin' stubborn about getting her way."

"Is she the only one who's being stubborn about things?"

Quinn straightened. "You saw how I was—I offered compromises. I try to work with her, but—"

"You offered compromises in the boss's office. Why didn't you offer those compromises before now?"

His mouth opened and closed a few times as he looked for an answer that didn't sound defensive. He rubbed a hand over the back of his neck.

"I don't know. I guess I assumed she'd shut me down. We seem to have this…*thing* between us."

"Oh?" Blake's heavy eyebrows rose dramatically. "What kind of thing?"

"Not *that* kind, brunch daddy." Quinn chuckled and stood, ignoring the curse word Blake tossed his way. "I'm not in the market, and I don't think she is, either."

"I don't know if she's *ever* had a serious relationship." Blake frowned. "Not that I'm into her personal life, but she *is* my wife's best friend, so I think I'd hear. She's always been hyperfocused on work and school." He stood and walked to the door with Quinn. "You aren't ready to start dating yet, huh?"

"No." His answer was quick, but he felt a weird quivering in his chest. He'd missed a woman's companionship since Anne died, but he'd had to focus on raising Katie. Now, though, Katie was getting ready for college, and he wouldn't have that excuse. Was it time to think about dating? The quiver turned into a shudder. "I don't know if I'll ever be ready. I've already had my soul mate, you know? It's unlikely there's another one out there for me."

"I'm sorry I never met your wife. I can't even imagine what that was like…losing her. I almost lost Amanda before we were married, and those hours in the hospital were some of the worst…" Blake put his hand on Quinn's shoulder. "But don't you think she'd want you to be happy again?"

"I *am* happy. I've raised a terrific kid. I've got a great job." He might not be on the tour anymore, but he really did like working and teaching at the Gallant Lake Golf Club. "I've got a nice house. A boat. Good friends. And I had my one great love. What more could I ask for?"

Blake looked like he wanted to say something else, then he clapped Quinn's shoulder again and told him to have a good afternoon.

Quinn headed down the ornate spiral staircase that anchored the three-story lobby at the resort. The stairs wrapped around a pillar designed to look like a tree trunk, and huge metal leaves hung from the ceiling and resembled a tree canopy. A few guests were gathered in seating areas near the huge windows overlooking the pool and the lake beyond it. Randall had done a hell of a job fixing this place up. He'd heard it was an outdated mash-up of 1940s Catskills kitsch and 1980s shiny brass when Blake bought it. Luckily he'd married an interior designer, scrapped the casino plans, and they'd turned the place into an upscale hotel.

He caught a blur of motion to his right as he neared the main floor. No surprise—it was Julie, going a hundred miles an hour as usual. He followed her toward the main reception desk, where she'd rushed up to an older woman with blue hair— literally—and a mountain of leather luggage behind her. She did not look pleased. Quinn stepped to the side, near a table sporting a huge floral arrangement, so as not to distract from what seemed to be a customer service crisis.

"Mrs. Pembleton, I'm *so* sorry for any confusion. Of *course*, we can accommodate your request for an end suite through this week and the weekend. The computer system had some sort of hiccup that didn't show your reservation, but we rebooted and…voilà!" Julie held up a hand as if revealing a magic trick. "There it was. If you could give us a few minutes to make sure the suite is ready for you, I'd truly appreciate it. I spoke with Chef Dario and he's going to whip up one of those watercress-and-lemon sandwiches you like so much while you wait. I'll have one of our bellhops take your luggage to the suite, and it'll be ready for you in…" She glanced at her watch. "Twenty minutes? Is that little scamp Pickles with you? Does he need anyone to take him for a walk?"

The older woman tried to hold on to her indignation, but when Julie mentioned *Pickles* her face lit up. "Oh, Julie, you're such a darling!" Quinn wasn't sure of the accent—it was a blend of London and Long Island. "Of course, Pickles is here—right in that top travel case. You know how he adores you. If you could take him outside while I eat my sandwich, I might forget about all this unpleasantness."

"I can't imagine anything I'd rather do than walk that cutie pie." Julie was practically gushing. Quinn's eyes narrowed. There was an undercurrent of falseness to it. But Mrs. Pembleton didn't seem to notice. She was already heading to a table near the windows, as if she just expected people to dash around catering to her desires.

Julie looked grim as she reached for the small

leather bag at the top of the luggage pile and pulled a tiny ball of black fluff from inside. A tiny *snarling* ball of fluff with flashing white teeth. Julie cooed at it, but he noticed she was careful to keep the… dog?…away from her face or any other body parts. She snapped on a leash, set him on the floor and headed toward the front door after giving a few quick instructions to the reception-desk staff.

Quinn didn't speak until she walked past him. "I didn't realize *dog walker* was one of your duties as manager."

Julie glanced over her shoulder toward Mrs. Pembleton as she shushed him. "Keep your voice down. If his momma thinks someone is disrespecting her little darling, we could lose her as a client. Surely you have golfers you wish weren't so demanding."

He could list half a dozen off the top of his head. He followed her outdoors. The dog yapped nonstop at everything and nothing.

"I suppose, but are you sure that lady is worth it?" He'd have told her to stuff it and her little dog, too.

Julie gave him a humorless grin. "There are times like today when I wonder, but…yes. Dolores Pembleton is ridiculously wealthy and she loves our resort. She holds an annual ladies' weekend here every fall with her bridge club and she pays for the whole thing. Plus she brings her family here around the holidays, *and* she surprises us with little get-aways like today."

"Surprises? She didn't have a lost reservation?"

Julie grimaced as Pickles did his business on the lawn. "Dammit, I don't have a bag... Oh, there's a dispenser on the leash. Now I just have to...ick." Quinn wordlessly took the bag from her hand and scooped up Pickles's waste, tying a quick knot in the bag to seal the odor. Julie's eyes went wide. "Nicely done."

"Katie had a labradoodle when she was younger, so I had plenty of practice."

"To answer your question," Julie said, turning back to the resort's entrance. "We had no idea she was coming. That happens sometimes, and she always insists she made reservations. And we always scramble and make it work. Thank God there was a suite open this week."

"Why does she do that?"

Julie looked back at him, her eyes softening. "I don't know for sure, but I suspect things aren't always happy at home with *Mr.* Pembleton. I think she runs away to us when she needs a break. Or to torture him. Or to torture us." She held the door for Pickles and looked back at Quinn as he dropped the poop bag in the outdoor trash container. "Who knows? It's all part of the job. I'm sorry, was there something you needed? Did Blake have any other suggestions after our meeting?"

"No. I was going to see if we could finalize the schedule together, but I can see you have your hands full."

She watched the little dog prancing around her ankles. "Yes, I do. Why don't I email you what we have so far, and I promise I'll be open to your feedback."

"Sounds good." He paused. "I'm glad we were able to figure things out earlier."

She stared at him for a minute, then her mouth slid into a smile. "I'm sure you are—you got your way with most of it. But you had a point about the importance of keeping the golfers happy that weekend. I'll do my best to stay in my lane."

Quinn had a feeling it took some effort for her to agree to that. "Same here."

Neither of them had apologized, but it felt like a truce of sorts. Watching Julie with that Pembleton woman, he saw her use not only smooth customer-service and business skills, but also compassion. There was more to her than the stubborn pride he kept bumping into.

In three years, today was the first time he'd seen Julie as something other than an irritant to his workday. Tomorrow might see them locking horns again, but at least he'd had that close-up glimpse of laughter and business savvy. As he climbed the steps to the clubhouse, he remembered she'd called him a *cinnamon roll*. That didn't do much for his own pride, that was for sure.

She said it meant *sweet*, which was okay. But it also meant *too good to be true*. Did that mean she didn't trust him? It was hardly a surprise, considering their territorial disputes at work, but the thought bothered him a lot more than it probably should.

Chapter Three

Julie walked into the Five and Design boutique with an armful of bridesmaid dresses encased in plastic bags. The infamous peacock dress was one of them, along with a kelly green gown and a slinky black sheath gown hemmed with pale pink ostrich feathers.

Melanie Brannigan and Amanda were huddled together at the counter, looking at a tablet propped against some boxes of cologne. Mel looked up when the bell rang above the door and rubbed her hands together in glee. "Are these the dresses? Luis! Come down here—our challenge has arrived!"

No one would guess Mel and Amanda were cousins. Mel was tall and slender, with long, dark hair.

Amanda was petite, blonde and curvy. Their other local cousin, Nora Peyton, was somewhere in between. The coffee-shop owner was petite, but had dark hair and eyes like Mel.

Mel was a former supermodel, and her business partner, Luis Alvarado, was the fashion designer every celebrity wanted to wear these days. They'd been staging fashion shows at the charity gala dinner in August for several years, with models wandering among the tables so guests could see the fashions up close. Every year was a different theme, like Sportswear Meets Couture, or Little Black Dresses Everywhere.

Amanda suggested they use Julie's dresses as inspiration for a theme based on reuse and recycle. Mel loved the idea and dubbed it Sustainable Style. In addition to some of Julie's dresses, they'd hit local secondhand shops to create showstopper looks both fancy and casual. It would inspire people to think before rushing to buy the "next new thing."

Julie was happy to donate some of her dresses to a good cause. Right now only a few of them could be worn without screaming *I'm wearing a bridesmaid dress!* And, except for the gown she'd worn at Amanda's wedding, she had no deep attachment to any of the dresses.

A large man rushed down the staircase from the formal-wear salon on the second floor. Luis looked more like a football player than a fashion designer.

He gave her a big smile that got even bigger when he saw the dresses Mel was laying out on the counter.

"Get. Out." He grabbed the sparkly peacock dress and held it up. "You did *not* wear this. And if you did, I must see you wearing it again. Like right now."

"No way." Julie shook her head adamantly. "That thing was too tight ten years ago."

They finally got her to agree—reluctantly—to try on as many of the dresses as possible so they had "before" photos to use at the show.

"Take selfies in a full-length mirror," Mel said. "Nothing fancy."

"Do you promise to cut off my head in the photos? I don't want to be plastered all over anyone's social media account." People were always taking pictures and videos at the show.

Mel pinkie-swore that she would not show Julie's face in any of the images. The little brass bell above the door rang out and they all turned as a man walked in. *Oh, my.* He was a George Clooney look-alike, with silver-tipped hair, a square jaw and what seemed like perpetually amused eyes. But this guy's eyes were blue, which only made him better-looking.

Luis mumbled, "Hello, hottie!" under his breath.

Julie answered in a whisper. "The hot ones are always taken."

"Welcome to Five and Design!" Mel walked over

to greet him. "Can I help you find anything? We have a men's section in the back left corner."

He shook his head with a smile that lit up his eyes. "I'm looking for a ladies' jacket. I was told to find something—" he made air quotes with his fingers "'—stylish but warm.' She wears a medium. And a scarf, too. A..." His eyebrows gathered together. The puzzled look did not affect his hotness one bit. "A pashmina? Whatever that is."

"See?" Julie muttered. "Taken."

Luis headed back upstairs, and Julie and Amanda watched Mel assist Mr. Hot But Taken. Once his purchases were bagged up in her signature dark blue bags with lots of pale blue tissue paper tumbling over the top, she brought him back to where Julie and Amanda were standing.

"Russell Gantry, I want you to meet a few of Gallant Lake's locals." She gestured toward them and made introductions. "Amanda and her husband own the Gallant Lake Resort, and Julie is their manager."

"Russell just bought a house up on the mountain, not far from Nora and Asher. His *sister* is here for the week to help him get settled in and give the place a woman's touch, but she didn't realize how chilly the Catskills can be this time of year."

Mel had emphasized the word *sister* and looked straight at Julie when she did. So...maybe not taken after all? Amanda had already jumped to her feet and extended her hand to Russell.

"Welcome to Gallant Lake! It's a great little town. Plenty to do, but still quiet and friendly."

Russell nodded, looking out the window to Main Street with its old-fashioned flag-festooned lampposts and the lake glistening beyond the businesses on the other side of the street.

"I can see that. We were at the coffee shop yesterday and met the owner, Nora. She's the one who told my sister about Mel's shop, but Lois woke up with a killer headache so she entrusted me with the mission." He held up the bag with a grin. "Hopefully she'll approve."

Julie smiled. "You can't go wrong in Mel's shop. How did you happen to find Gallant Lake, Russell?"

"Please, call me Russ. I work from home and it was time to get out of Manhattan." He winked. "And away from my ex." *Definitely available.* "The city gets small when you don't want to run into your past—and their new husband—everywhere you go. My sister came to a wedding here and thought it would be perfect for me. Not too far from the city, but with some skiing in the winter and golf courses in the summer."

"Oh!" Amanda's eyes went wide. "Our friend's husband owns the ski resort."

Russ smiled. "One of my favorite golfers is living here, too." He turned to Julie. "Wait…if you run the resort, does that mean Quinn Walker works for you?"

Her laughter was louder than she'd intended. "My life would be easier if he did, but no. He runs the golf club. I run the hotel and spa." She swallowed her laughter. "But we *do* work together. Do you know him?"

"No, but I'm a huge fan. I love the game of golf, and I admire guys like Walker who take the game seriously. Do you play?"

"Me?" Julie put her hand on her chest. "I—"

"Of course, she does!" Amanda exclaimed.

What the...?

Mel jumped right in. "Not as much as she'd like, with her job and all, but she gets out there on the fairways. My husband has seen her."

Julie's face heated. The last time Shane Brannigan saw Julie walking the course in the evening, he'd gently warned her how strict Quinn was about not allowing nongolfers anywhere near his precious manicured course. Especially anyone wearing jeans. She had no idea why anyone thought a game so full of archaic rules could be fun.

She'd started to say as much when Russ gave her a drop-dead-gorgeous smile. This guy was the real deal, between that smile and those silver-blue eyes. "That's great! We should definitely play a round together."

She knew he meant a round of golf, but the other idea sounded pretty good, too. There was only one problem. "I'm pretty bad at it." Translation: she'd never played.

"Don't be silly!" Amanda insisted. "Blake told me you're *filled* with potential." Everyone other than Russ knew Blake only used that phrase when someone had no talent at all. It was his subtle way of saying the person had nowhere to go but up.

"Don't worry," Russ chuckled. "Your skill level isn't as important as your love for the game. If you've got that, the rest will come with practice. I can give you some tips."

"Give him your card, Julie!" Mel nudged her. The cousins were definitely trying to jump-start her dating life. It would be cute if it wasn't so humiliating. But Julie fished out a card from her wallet, anyway.

"Here you go. I, uh, have a full schedule for the next month or so, but when things calm down I'll take you up on that golf game." Once she learned how to play. This guy might just be worth the effort.

Their fingers touched briefly as he took the cards. "I'd like that. Maybe we can grab dinner before then so you can tell me about Gallant Lake."

"Um…" Julie flinched when Mel's elbow poked her in the back. "Yeah. Maybe."

After he'd headed out of the shop, Mel and Amanda were literally aflutter with excitement.

"Holy hot new guy!" Amanda laughed. "You were saying the other day that you'd dated everyone in town at least once, but you haven't dated *this* guy."

"He is a looker," Mel agreed. "Great manners, too. Friendly. No creepy vibes. Looking for a fresh start.

By the way, he told me he doesn't have children, so no messy complications now that he's divorced."

Julie couldn't argue with any of that. Russ Gantry checked all the boxes. Other than the lack of any sizzle between them. But that might develop over time.

"If you're really sick of being a bridesmaid all the time," Amanda said, "take a chance and see where it goes."

Mel agreed. "If the golf thing worries you that much, take some lessons from Quinn."

"Oh, yeah, that would be great." Julie groaned, sliding her bag over her shoulder. "We're always at odds, and you want me to put myself in a submissive situation where he'd be the teacher? Thanks, but no thanks."

Amanda's eyebrows rose. "*Submissive* is an interesting choice of words. Just because he's giving you lessons doesn't mean he's in charge. You're the client. He'd be working for you for once."

She had a point. Quinn might be giving the instructions, but she'd be the one with the final say. And he certainly wouldn't want her complaining to Blake that the lessons weren't going well.

"And," Amanda pointed out, "even if you decide Russ isn't for you, at least you'll know a bit more about the game of golf. It might break the ice between you and Quinn. And as resort manager, it wouldn't hurt for you to at least know the lingo of the game."

Another good point. *Damn it.* Looked like she was going to take some golf lessons. From Quinn. Ugh.

"Of all the golf joints in all the world, you had to walk into mine." It was a bad ad-lib, but Quinn got caught off guard when he looked up from the computer and saw Julie walk into the pro shop. She wandered through the racks of golf attire, all sporting the golf club's logo. She looked completely put together, as always. Hair tucked behind her ears. Slim black slacks and a pale blue knit top with small ruffles on the collar and on the short sleeves. A few discrete glimmers of gold jewelry. Practical walking shoes—it seemed the woman never sat down during working hours. Hardly any makeup. Just a soft coral sheen on her lips and what looked like a natural pink glow on her cheeks as she ran her hand over the new inventory of summer golf shirts for ladies.

Quinn blinked. Why was he cataloging her looks like that? He cleared his throat sharply, bringing her attention snapping in his direction. "Uh…did we have a meeting I forgot about?"

"No," she answered. She didn't elaborate, looking away again. Everything in her body language screamed she didn't want to be here, but…here she was. In his pro shop. Where she'd been maybe four times since he'd started working here.

"Is there something I can help you with?"

She hesitated, then looked his way again. "You do lessons, right?"

"*Golf* lessons? Well, it's my job, so…yeah." Had someone complained about a class? "Is there a problem I need to know about?"

"No…sorry." She finally walked over to the counter to face him. "I'm not sure why I'm doing this, but…do you think you could give me lessons?"

"*Golf* lessons?" He blurted the words out again. Julie had never expressed any interest in, or respect for, the game of golf.

"Unless there's something else you teach, yes, I'd like golf lessons."

"Why?" He thought of their meeting a few days earlier. "Was this Blake's idea? Because I can talk to him and—"

"Is the thought of giving me a couple golf lessons that terrible?"

"No!" He actually had no idea what that would be like. Annoying? Challenging? Maybe fun? *Nah. Probably not that one.* "Now I'm the one who's sorry. Of course, I can set you up for some lessons. It's just— I thought you hated golf."

"I do. I mean… I've always said I did, but someone suggested it might open me up to more opportunities to…meet people."

Quinn frowned. "I'm not saying that doesn't happen, but golf is a fairly solitary sport. It's you against the course, if you know what I mean."

She looked exasperated with him. "What about all that business that supposedly happens on the golf course?"

"Well…yeah. Businesspeople can have conversations on the links that lead to business deals. It can build a sense of trust and camaraderie when you're riding in a cart with the same person for four hours." He smiled in understanding. She was showing her business savvy again. "And you don't want to miss out on those conversations, is that it? Build rapport with guests and local bigwigs over a round of golf and maybe a beer afterward? Makes sense."

She started to speak, stopped, then started again with a quick nod. "Yes. That's it exactly. Camaraderie. That's what I want." Her cheeks went a deeper shade of pink for some reason. "And it might help me understand some of the things golfers expect when they come to a resort for tournaments. Learn the lingo and all that."

"If you can't beat 'em, join 'em, huh?"

"What? Oh… I get it." She laughed, but it didn't ring sincere. "For one thing, it's never been about beating you… Okay, maybe *some* arguments were about winning. Consider this a peace offering of sorts. I'm trying to learn your viewpoint."

"And what do I get out of this? A day as resort manager?"

She rolled her eyes. "You get to boss me around during each lesson. Isn't that enough?"

"It is, actually." He pulled up his schedule on the computer screen. "How about Monday morning?"

"I'm off on Mondays."

"Were you planning on taking your class during working hours?"

"Good point. What time? I am not giving up my Monday-morning sleep-in." Ah, so she *did* relax sometimes.

"That means the nine-o'clock slot is out. How about eleven?"

"Fine."

Quinn huffed out a soft laugh. "You don't have to make it sound like you're about to be tortured."

"We'll see. What do I need to bring?"

"I'm assuming you don't have any equipment of your own?" Her startled expression was all the answer he needed. "Don't worry about it. Sneakers with a good tread will work for the first few lessons, and I have loaner clubs here you can use. If you last longer than a few lessons, we'll set you up with what you need. Wear something comfortable, but no sweats, jeans or T-shirts. The club rules apply to students, too."

She rolled her eyes again, and Quinn held back a chuckle. She could give Katie a run for her money in the eye-rolling category.

"And you wonder why I think golf is a stuffy old sport. I'll see you Monday."

"At which time I'll try to change your mind about the game."

"Good luck with that!"

After she left, Quinn wondered at her change of heart about golfing. He didn't know her that well, but all her talk about *business* and *learning the lingo* rang false to him. Whatever her reasons, she'd be showing up for a lesson on Monday. If they could avoid arguing, it might give them a chance to know each other better. Which would be good for their professional relationship.

But could they avoid arguing for an entire forty-minute lesson, where it would be only the two of them? Only time would tell.

Chapter Four

Julie stared at her reflection in the mirror and made a face. She wasn't exactly an example of "golf chic," but she looked okay. Boring, but Quinn had made such a fuss about *no denim* and *the rules* that she'd been a bit paranoid about what to wear. It had been on the cool side lately, so she'd pulled on a pair of chinos and a light sweater worn over a polo shirt. Apparently collars were a big deal in golf, although what that had to do with playing the game was a mystery.

She stuffed her hair under a Gallant Lake Resort cap and turned away before she started overthinking again. This was a golf lesson, not a performance at Carnegie Hall. Forty minutes of swinging a golf club and then it would be over. She walked out to the kitchen and rinsed her coffee mug in the sink before putting down some kibble for Fluff and heading out the door. The cat was aggressively independent. She ate when she wanted and demanded attention when she wanted. And woe to anyone who touched her when she *didn't* want it.

As soon as she was finished with Quinn, she was going to the grocery store for the fixings for another recipe from that old cookbook of German foods. Her brother, Bobby, was coming over for dinner later with his new lady friend, and when she told him she was pretty sure she'd found a recipe identical to Nanny's beef rolls, he'd begged her to make it.

Their great-grandmother had been the only semblance of stability in their chaotic upbringing. Nanny Rueckert hadn't moved from Brooklyn to Gallant Lake until after their father left for good. Mom had been on one of her many roller-coaster rides between sober depression and drunken unpredictability, and Nanny realized her great-grandchildren needed her. She'd been eighty at the time. Bobby and Julie had clung to her like she was a life raft. Her little apartment above one of the shops on Main Street was where they headed after school for hugs, wisdom and homemade German pastries.

They'd walk home for dinner, but if Mom had

spent her afternoon drinking rather than cooking, as happened on a regular basis, the two of them would walk right back to Nanny's for a meal and perhaps to stay the night. It was only her mother's foolhardy pride that kept her from allowing her children to move in full-time with Nanny Rueckert. And letting her grandmother move into *their* home was too much for Mom. She probably didn't want her to see who she really was, as if the whole town hadn't already figured that one out.

Nanny had done the best she could to provide a safe haven for Bobby and Julie. She almost always had an apron on, and even now Julie remembered the smell of spices and yeast in her kitchen. Amanda often teased her about her love for cooking being about the ability to control something, and that was partially true. But it was more than that. It was a tangible connection to the woman who'd helped her figure out how to become a functioning adult despite a stressful childhood and the crippling self-doubt she'd been left with.

Nanny died a year after Julie graduated high school. Her strong-willed great-grandmother had been eighty-six but had still been trudging up a long flight of stairs to that second-floor apartment, cooking the same comfort food and offering up the same hugs, even if they felt a bit more frail. Julie had moved in with her at seventeen and kept the apartment for years after Nanny passed.

She pulled into the resort and took the side road toward the golf club. This was such a silly idea. Russ was a catch, but he probably wouldn't want anything serious with Julie even if she *did* know how to golf. She'd told Amanda last night that she had too much baggage for most men and too little patience to deal with *their* baggage. She'd never been one to pretend to be someone she wasn't, and she was not a golfer. She was surprised to see Quinn waiting for her on the wide veranda by the front entrance.

"Am I late?" she asked as she got out of the car.

He glanced at his watch. "Right on time. I saw your car headed this way and figured we could walk straight over to the driving range."

"Well, aren't you efficient?"

He grinned. "You don't have to sound *that* surprised."

They went across the parking lot to the driving range, away from the more valuable lake views and tucked into a clearing in the trees. Quinn wasn't carrying any golf clubs. When he saw her looking around, he explained he'd already taken everything she needed to the range. So…this was really happening. She was going to learn how to golf. How hard could it be? One session would probably be enough for her to be able to start playing. She had to learn how to aim the ball and hit it more often than not, and she'd be all set.

"It's not like I'm planning to go pro." She blurted

out her final thought when she saw the sunny yellow golf bag with green tapestry inserts. The colors were soft—no screaming golf plaids in sight. It was the kind of golf bag Julie might pick for herself if she ever went that far. It was filled with what seemed to be way too many golf clubs.

"I'm glad to hear it," Quinn answered with a bemused expression. "That would be a long shot considering you don't know the game."

"Then why do I need all these different golf clubs?"

"I put a few different lengths and flex shafts in there to see what works best." He smiled at her confusion. "You can't have this many clubs in your bag when you play in any sanctioned events. We'll pare it down after today's session."

"Yeah, I'm not going to need more than three or four clubs. I just want to be able to play the game."

Quinn started to laugh. "You can't play the game with three or four clubs. Trust me." He crossed his arms across his chest. "What *do* you know about golf?"

"That it's a game played by a bunch of old men with horrendous taste in clothes who take the rules and themselves *way* too seriously."

His eyebrows rose under the brim of his golf cap until she couldn't see them anymore. "That's your very one-sided *opinion* about *golfers*. Now tell me what you know about the *game* of golf. Have you really never played?"

"Does miniature golf count?"

"Not much, but at least you've held a putter in your hand and understand the concept of getting the ball in the hole." He handed her a long club with a bulbous turquoise head on the end. "But today isn't about putting. I want to see you swing a club, but first, stand back and watch me hit a few."

He grabbed a silver-and-white golf club from his own well-worn bag and stepped up, putting a ball on a rubber tee. He motioned again for her to stand back, then took a swing. For some reason, Julie had always thought of golf as a nonphysical sport. Take the little stick and swing it at the little ball. But when she heard the *whoosh* of Quinn's golf club whipping through the air and the sharp *ping* of it hitting the ball, which rocketed off the tee and flew through the air so far and so fast she immediately lost track of it…well, that was definitely physical. Then he did it again. And again.

And speaking of physical, the way Quinn's body coiled and released as he swung was…impressive. Even when he'd annoyed her, she'd always admitted two facts about Quinn Walker. He was a devoted dad to Katie, and he was built like a superhero—all corded muscles and rippling shoulders, with thick, wavy hair. The type of guy she'd often mocked as being too pretty to be real. But damn, he'd look good in a skintight bodysuit and a cape...

"So." His voice shook her out of her musing. "What do you think? Ready to give it a try?"

"How fast is that thing going?" She pointed to where the ball flew out over the driving range, with its white signs identifying yardage. One hundred. One-fifty. Two hundred.

"An amateur golfer swings the club head at about ninety miles an hour. The pros hit it closer to the one-ten range. A pro can send a golf ball from zero to a hundred and fifty miles an hour." He set another ball on the tee.

"You're telling me this sport is actually *dangerous*?" Did she really want to be anywhere near a rock-hard ball going a hundred and fifty miles per hour? What kind of liability did something like that bring to the resort? She made a mental note to check their insurance policy.

"Don't tell me you're afraid of all us badly dressed old men." He stepped away from the golf ball and gestured for her to step up to the tee. "But it can be dangerous if you're not completely aware of your surroundings at all times. You don't want to walk into someone's backswing, and you sure don't want to be hit by a ball, especially as it's coming off the clubhead."

"I thought golf was supposed to be relaxing. I've seen it on TV a few times when my brother was watching a tournament, and it never looked death-defying. Maybe it was that weird whispering the announcers do that makes it feel so... I don't know... *Not* deadly?"

Quinn gripped his club and held it up so she could see where his fingers were. She did her best to imitate him with her own club. He nudged her shoulder gently with a chuckle before stepping away.

"It's not like it's Thunderdome out on the golf course every day. You just have to pay attention. You're a stickler for detail, so you should be fine at that. Now take a swing at the ball."

She felt a stab of anxiety at his stickler-for-detail comment. Was that supposed to be a jab? Or a compliment? She was used to fending off the former, but she had a harder time handling the latter. Rather than ask about it, she focused her attention on the tiny white golf ball. She did her best to copy his stance when he was swinging—feet apart, bent at the waist, arms extended down to the club. All she had to do was swing the club and smack that ball.

She swung as hard as she could, spinning herself around and stumbling a step to catch her balance. Sadly, the golf ball was still sitting on the tee. She'd missed! She quickly set up to try again, but Quinn grabbed the club before she could start her swing.

"Whoa! Remember what I said about being aware of your surroundings. I was walking up to you."

"Why? Just stand back there and let me figure this out."

A flash of annoyance crossed his face.

"Feel free to come here and swing at golf balls all day long. But if you want to *learn*, step back and let me teach you. That's what you're paying for, remember?"

For the next half hour, he showed her how she was supposed to stand, how her arm was supposed to be straight, how the club was supposed to move in a perfect arc so that when she pulled it back and swung, it would *move through the ball*, whatever that meant. Follow through with her hips. Don't swing too hard, but if she swung too soft she wouldn't be able to control the ball. Don't stand up. Keep her eyes on the ball at all times. She did manage to connect the golf club and the ball together a few times, but she had more misses than hits, and even the better hits dribbled onto the range instead of coming anywhere near flying the way his balls did.

She finally turned to him in exasperation, one hand on her hip. "You're punking me, aren't you? This game is a joke."

He'd been leaning over his club to demonstrate what she was doing wrong, and he looked up in surprise. "What do you mean?"

"There is no way on God's green earth that a person can remember all of that gobbledygook. And if they *did*, how could this game possibly be considered *fun*?" She dropped the golf club into the yellow bag. "All I want is to be able to not make a fool of myself. I don't need to know all the fancy stuff."

"I hate to break this to you, but we haven't even come close to the *fancy stuff* yet." He put his own golf club in his bag. "I know it sounds like a lot, but once you get the basic swing down and commit it to muscle memory, the rest of it will start to make more sense. I've probably let you do too many swings today. Your shoulders will be aching in the morning."

"I doubt it," she scoffed. "I keep myself in very good shape." *Very* might be an exaggeration, but she used the gym at the resort four days a week and liked to hike and go cycling.

Quinn seemed to take a long, measured breath. Was he losing patience with her?

"I don't care if you're the strongest woman in the world. This game uses different muscles. All I'm saying is don't be surprised if you have a few aches tomorrow. For homework, I want you—"

"Homework?" Julie pulled back, still stinging from his strongest-woman comment. "There's *homework* for golf lessons? All I have to do is connect the club with the ball. I think I can figure that out without homework."

His lips slid into a hard line. Yup—he was annoyed. They were back to their normal adversarial stance. She didn't mind. It was what she was used to.

"Look." Quinn's eyes narrowed dangerously. "If this game is that simple, why are you here? If anyone here should feel like they're being punked, it's *me*. You obviously expect to become magically competent at a game you have no respect for without putting in any of the work. I don't know what motivated you to take lessons, but if you're not going to work at it, don't waste my time."

Her whole body went still. Even her lungs seemed to pause. She'd never been good at hearing criticism, especially from men. And Quinn had just used a whole bunch of trigger words. She could hear her mother's voice in her head. *You never listen. You're lazy. Stupid. You want motivation? I'll give you some damn motivation—come here...*

"Julie? I didn't mean..." Quinn's voice was softer now, edged with regret. She couldn't look at him. She was usually able to control her reactions, but right now she didn't trust herself not to break and either burst into tears, or rip into him in a screaming tirade. It had been a long time since she'd done either, but Quinn managed to break through her usual defenses. That realization shook her.

"I've gotta go." She pushed past him, swatting at his hand when he tried to grip her arm. "Don't do that. Just... I need to go. Sorry." She mumbled the last word and kicked herself for it. Apologizing to scolding adults had been her fallback position since she was five. *Sorry, Daddy. Sorry, Mommy. Please don't be mad.*

She broke into a near jog toward her car, ignoring Quinn's voice calling after her. He watched in obvious confusion as she drove off. To his credit, he didn't try to stop her. She held herself together until she was off resort property and on the main road, then she cried all the way home. She needed to stuff all the ugliness back into the mental vault and pull herself together.

And then she'd have to figure out a way to never, *ever* face Quinn Walker again.

Chapter Five

The sound of the roasting pan hitting the stainless steel sink echoed in the kitchen. With the wide-open floor plan of the contemporary lakefront house, it echoed through the whole place. Katie called down from upstairs, leaning over the hallway railing.

"Are you remodeling down there? Taking down a wall? Smashing cabinets with a sledgehammer?"

Quinn checked the sink for dents and breathed a sigh of relief before he answered.

"Sorry, honey. I don't know my own strength, I guess."

He heard her footsteps coming down the stairs. "Dad, you've been banging things around for two days. Last night I heard you throw your shoes across your room like a five-year-old." Katie came into the kitchen, pulling her long hair into a scrunchie as she walked. Her denim shorts were so short they were nearly invisible under her T-shirt. Sometimes Quinn felt she was trying to give him a heart attack with her fashion choices, but she was a young woman now and he had to pick his battles. She walked over and put her hand on his forearm. Damn if she didn't naturally do things exactly like her mom had. "Is there something we need to talk about?"

He swallowed the lump of emotion in his throat. "I'm still not used to *you* being the grown-up around here. Sorry about the noise last night. I, uh, dropped one of my shoes."

She shook her head and laughed. "Bull. I know what thrown shoes sound like. It was one of my specialties as a fifteen-year-old, remember?"

He did. Fifteen had been a fun time in this house. Anne had been gone just over a year. He'd uprooted Katie from their home in Ponte Vedra, Florida, and brought her here so he could take the job at the resort. It had given him fairly regular hours and a good income. The school system was supposed to be excellent, if much smaller than what Katie was used to. Thanks to the difference in housing costs, he'd been able to get a smaller but comfortable house right on the water. It was supposed to be a fresh start for both of them.

But he'd underestimated the trauma of plucking a teenage girl from her circle of friends at a time like that. To say she'd been unhappy about it would be a vast understatement. More than shoes had flown through the air those first six months or so. Accusations. Books. A lamp. He'd bungled things, but with the help of a family counselor they'd made it through.

"Dad, you're starting to worry me. What's up? Did you get fired or something?"

"What? No! Why would you think I got fired?"

"What else could it be? Unless you have a dating-app profile I don't know about, you're not involved with anyone, so it's not a lover's spat. And you're obviously scorched about something. Who fried your toast?"

"*I* did. I'm mad at myself, Kate. I said something that hurt someone, but I have no idea what it was that set her off. I don't know how to fix it."

"*Her?*" Katie tugged him to the kitchen island and pointed at the chrome bar stools. "Sit. And spill."

Talking to his teenage daughter about this felt... weird. But, as he kept reminding himself, Katie was a woman now and he could use a woman's perspective. He sat with a heavy sigh. Was this the beginning of old age? When he turned to his offspring for help?

"I was giving a golf lesson to Julie Brown—"

"*The* Julie Brown? The woman you never agree with on anything? Why on earth are you giving her lessons?"

That was a really good question. "She asked for lessons, and she runs the resort. Turning her down didn't seem like a great idea."

"But Dad…she *hates* golf."

"She made that pretty clear. She's doing it to meet people or something. She wasn't serious about it, but she didn't have bad form. Then things fell apart and I don't know what happened or how to fix it." He looked at Katie. "I think I *really* hurt her feelings somehow. She got upset all of a sudden, then she bolted."

Quinn told Katie about the lesson. Julie's digs about golf and golfers in general, particularly once he mentioned homework—which was only going to be a few stretches so she didn't hurt herself. And, yes, he'd lost his patience when she mocked the game that had bought this house and allowed him to raise his daughter. He'd fired back, but dammit, *she'd* started it. And they'd always had that back-and-forth snark. He figured Julie would just give it right back to him.

But the way the color drained from her face? The devastation in her eyes? It was out of proportion to what had happened, and he hadn't known how to respond. Everything went upside down, and he was left feeling guilty without knowing what he was guilty of.

"Dad…" Katie's expression was a mix of surprise and disappointment. "What have you always taught me about disagreeing with someone?"

He frowned. "I don't know… Be nice?"

She rolled her eyes dramatically. It was her special talent. "You've always told me to criticize the *ideas* or *actions* I disagreed with, not attack the person themselves."

"Yeah, that sounds like something I'd say." He gave her a quick grin to break the tension, remembering the lectures he'd given her. "Argue about opinions rather than personalities."

"Apparently it's something you say, but don't do."

"What are you talking about?"

"Dad. Julie made fun of *golf*. The funny clothes. The old-white-dude stereotype." She leaned toward him, her eyes sad. He realized with a jolt that she was…*disappointed* in him. That stung. "And you reacted by telling her she was lazy, unmotivated and that you didn't want to teach her anymore."

"No! That's not what I…" He thought back. "But I didn't *mean* it that way. And I didn't call her lazy." He'd only said she didn't want to put in the work. *Damn it to hell.*

"Julie is always so cool and in control. You must have really triggered something. Dad, you've got to apologize to her. The sooner, the better."

"I don't know what I'm…" Katie fixed him with a firm look. Yeah, he had a much better idea now of what he'd done to hurt her feelings. "How did you get so smart, kiddo?"

She stood, planting a quick kiss on the top of his head. "Years of therapy, remember? Go apologize. Right now."

"It's after seven. She's already home…"

"So?" Katie was putting her earbuds back in place as she walked away, scrolling through her phone. "Don't give her another night to stew over what *you* did. It'll only make it worse."

Julie pulled a few more dresses out of the bridesmaid closet to take photos of so she could deliver them to Mel tomorrow.

As Mel had threatened at the boutique, they wanted photos of Julie wearing each of the dresses in order to have "before" images for the presentation at the Travis Foundation gala the weekend of the event. They'd agreed she could take them in front of her full-length mirror, and promised that her face would *not* appear in any of the photos. Just the dresses.

She'd been choosing a few dresses every couple of days to photograph, then delivered them to Mel and Luis. First up tonight was a baby blue gown with a satin top and billowing tulle ballroom skirt dotted with spots of glitter that had been attached with a hot glue gun. Julie remembered the party her friend Joy had held with all the bridesmaids, and the surprise when it turned out to be a let's-decorate-our-dresses! party. Julie had burned three of her fingertips that night, but the wine and laughter had been flowing freely. It wasn't anything she'd wear again by choice, but the dresses had looked sweet at the wedding and reflected her friend's artistic style. She couldn't help twirling in it before snapping a picture.

Next up was a dark green velvet gown with full-length puffed sleeves and a high neckline, trimmed in white lace. She'd worn it at a holiday wedding for an acquaintance many years ago—the dress had lasted far longer than the marriage had. She'd even kept the white fur hand muffs the bridesmaids had carried instead of flowers. The wedding photos looked like a Victorian Christmas card.

She pulled out a shiny hot pink floor-length satin sheath last. It had a wide band of sparkling crystals of various colors around the plunging neckline. The dress was from a friend's wedding ten years ago. Like the other two dresses, it wasn't a *bad* dress. It was just so obviously a bridesmaid's dress and so *not* her style, with the incandescent color and all the big, multicolor crystals at the neckline. She wondered if it would fit. Her figure hadn't changed much through the years, but this wedding had happened during her slimmest phase.

The resort had been in major financial trouble and on the market, and Julie had been in full-on panic mode over losing the only employer she'd known. She'd been so anxious that she'd forget to eat half the time. Those scary few years were what eventually propelled her to go after her college degree, and now her master's. She didn't ever want to feel that helpless again.

She could skip the tight pink dress, but trying on the dresses was a welcome distraction from thinking about Quinn and that horrid lesson. She still hadn't figured out how she was going to work with the man.

She stepped into the pink dress and pulled it up. Yeah…it was going to be tight. The design was form-fitting to start with, and her form at almost forty was not the same as at thirty. With a little shimmying, she got it on and managed to get her arms in the cap sleeves. With more twisting and reaching—and one brief moment of panic that she was stuck—she managed to get the full-length zipper almost all the way up. Far enough to quickly snap a few photos…as she prayed the seams wouldn't burst. Her reflection in the mirror looked like Jessica Rabbit—all curves and cleavage.

It wasn't until she went to remove the dress that the real trouble started. Twisting herself into a pretzel to reach behind her back and get her fingers on the zipper pull, Julie couldn't budge it. She tried reaching over her shoulder, thinking she could push it down, but that didn't work, either. Well, this was ridiculous. There had to be a way out of this. She reached behind her back again and pulled hard on the zipper...and the zipper pull broke off into her hand.

Now what?

The situation was so absurd she started to laugh, but the dress was too tight to allow it. Right behind the laughter were tears. *Trapped in a bridesmaid gown—this is how I go out.*

A knock on the front door at this hour would normally make her suspicious. But when she heard the sound now, she felt nothing but relief. Someone who could get her out of her predicament was here. She hurried to the door. It was probably Amanda or Cassie. Or Mel—she'd said she might stop by to look at all the dresses. It didn't matter *who* it was, as long as they could get her out of this damn dress.

She pulled open the door, her hair swinging across her face. "You couldn't have shown up at a better time!"

When she brushed back her hair and saw Quinn Walker standing there, all she could do was stare at him, dumbfounded. His expression mirrored what she imagined hers was—wide, surprised eyes, arching eyebrows and mouth open but making no sound. He cleared his throat awkwardly.

"Uh, clearly you're expecting someone else. I'll

just go… Sorry. We'll talk tomorrow." He started to turn away, then glanced at the skintight dress. "You look, uh, nice." He cleared his throat again. Or was that a choking sound? "Good night."

He was at the bottom of the front steps before she snapped out of her shock and remembered she was trapped in a dress.

"Wait!" she called out. "I don't know why you showed up at my front door, but I need you."

Quinn's eyebrows rose and she rushed to clarify her words. "I mean, I need your help. You have to get me out of this dress…"

At that moment, Mrs. Blumenthal from three houses down walked by. She was a lovely woman, but incredibly interested in what her neighbors were doing. Never maliciously, but she had a genuine, constant curiosity. Her timing couldn't have been worse. She stopped on the sidewalk, taking in Julie dressed in the clinging gown, telling a man that he needed to take off her dress. It would be perfect gossip fodder for after church this Sunday.

"Hi, Mrs. Blumenthal!" Julie waved with a big smile. "We're rehearsing a skit for an event at the resort. Did it sound real?"

"Well, you definitely gave me a start!" The older woman laughed. "You never have gentleman callers at the house, and to greet one dressed like Marilyn Monroe is definitely out of character for you."

Julie forced herself to laugh. "Well, thanks for

the compliment on looking like Marilyn." *And for announcing that the neighbors think I'm a dateless spinster.* "This is one of the employees from the resort." She gestured toward Quinn dismissively, inferring he worked *for* her, not with her. His eyes narrowed, but he stayed silent as she spoke to him for her neighbor's benefit. "Come inside and we'll work on the next skit. Good night, Mrs. Blumenthal!"

Quinn obediently walked into the house, taking care not to touch her as he went through the doorway. Mrs. Blumenthal waved back and headed down the sidewalk, humming to herself. Julie closed the front door behind Quinn and leaned against it with a heavy sigh, her eyes closed tightly against this disaster of an evening. Then she remembered Quinn Walker was *in her house* and her eyes snapped open again.

"What on earth are you doing here at this hour? How did you find my address?" The memory of their last meeting at that golf lesson made her cheeks flame. "What makes you think I want you in my house?"

"Hey, I'm only *in* your house because you demanded it. I'm more than happy to leave..." He reached for the doorknob, but she stopped him.

"Wait! You can't go until you unzip me."

Chapter Six

Quinn found the idea oddly enticing, but…no. "Unless you're talking about opening a zip file on your computer, forget it. We're coworkers and I remember all my HR training. It's bad enough I came to your house in the first place, but I just wanted to apologize for the other day…"

"Apologize? You don't need…"

"Julie, I got way too prickly. I took things personally, and even worse, I *made* it personal." He leveled his gaze on her wide eyes. Damn, that dress was a distraction, but her eyes were even more compelling, chocolate shot through with gold. He cleared his throat. "It was unprofessional and rude. I didn't want to wait another minute to tell you how sorry I am." *Don't look at that plunging neckline.* "As far as how I know where you live… I asked my daughter. And now, I really need to go back home…"

"You can't leave me standing here in this dress."

Every time she mentioned removing the dress, it hit him in a part of his chest that hadn't felt anything in years. The part that very much wanted to see Julie Brown out of that dress. *No, no, no.*

"You keep saying that, and I have no idea what you mean." There was no way it meant what he hoped.

She grimaced, then turned away from him, gesturing toward her back. "I was trying it on and the zipper broke. I can't get it off and it is hellishly tight and uncomfortable." She looked at him over her shoulder. "Please?"

Well, he couldn't leave her there stuck in that sexy dress, could he? From behind her, the view was just as enticing as the front. The bright pink fabric clung to every curve. *Hoo, boy.* He stepped closer and told her to hold still. He figured the zipper was just stuck, but she was right—it was broke. The tab had broken clean off, and the teeth of the zipper were not lined up properly. He tugged on it and muttered to himself until finally the teeth lined up again. But the zipper was still locked firmly in place.

He moved in closer to get his fingers under what was left of the zipper key, letting out a long sigh of frustration. It wasn't until Julie trembled that he realized he'd just sent his breath across the base of her neck…which was inches from his mouth. How had he gotten this close? Why were there tiny goose bumps on her ivory skin? Did she always smell this good?

"Everything okay back there?"

"Uh…what?"

"The *zipper*?"

The question was reasonable. But his brain short-circuited a bit when she spoke in a low, breathy voice he'd never heard from Julie before. He finally reined in his wildly scattering thoughts and cleared his throat, tugging again at the zipper while staring at a spot directly behind her ear. He could see her pulse racing. He was pretty sure his heart was matching it beat for beat.

When the zipper finally broke free in his hand, Quinn's mouth was very nearly touching that tender spot on Julie's neck. The sudden movement made both of them flinch, and he forced himself to step back to allow some space between them. Because a few seconds ago, there hadn't been any space at all. Had she leaned back into him, or had he pressed forward? It didn't matter. They just needed it to not happen again.

"Oh, my God, that feels so good!" There was something in the way she said it—the words themselves—and the feeling of his fingers still brushing the skin of her back. It all shot straight to another area on his body that hadn't perked up in a very long time. He closed his eyes and thought about the storage room behind the pro shop at the club that was an absolute mess and needed to be organized this weekend. The image worked almost as well as a cold shower.

"I aim to please." Did that sound suggestive? He forced his fingers away from her skin, curling them into a fist at his side. "I mean... I'm glad I could help."

Julie turned with a bright smile, and the tension in the room eased. They were a few feet apart now, and all that touching and breathing and pulse-watching was over. Except...now that plunging neckline plunged even farther. One strap had slipped off her shoulder and the dress was sagging dangerously. She didn't seem to notice, too busy breathing deeply and laughing—neither of which helped the neckline situation. He was pretty sure she was headed toward a wardrobe malfunction.

Don't look. Don't look. Don't look.

"Before you showed up, I thought I was going to have to call someone to come rescue me." Julie put her hand on her stomach, still not seeming to notice the impending exposure of her nicely rounded breasts. *Don't look!* She shook her head and chuckled. "It was either that or cut myself out of it, and I promised Mel I wouldn't damage any of the dresses before she had a chance to work her magic."

The weight of the beading around the neckline was pulling the dress ever lower. Another half inch and she'd have what those fashion shows Katie watched referred to as a nip slip. His mouth went dry as gravity continued to do its job.

"Uh, you should, uh… The dress is… The neckline, uh…" He spun around to face the door and closed his eyes tightly, knowing he had absolutely no right to witness the inevitable. "Your top…it's falling…"

"Oh!" Julie gasped. "Oh, no…oh, my God." He heard the dress being adjusted behind him. "This damn dress is cursed, and I need to get out of it right now."

Right now? Had that been the sound of the dress falling to the floor? He immediately started thinking of that storage room again. And doing inventory. Yeah…the idea of doing inventory would solve this embarrassing problem. "No, please…" He was begging now. "Let me leave first."

"Stay, Quinn." She put her hand flat on his back. "I'm going to run and change into something that will behave better than this thing, but I at least owe you a cup of coffee." She paused, amusement creeping into her voice again. "You can open your eyes now."

He did as she asked and found her standing off to his side, watching his face. The dress was back in place, held there with one hand to be safe.

"Go have a seat at the kitchen table." She nodded her head toward the kitchen. "I'll be out in a jiffy."

"I don't think I should—"

"You have to." She shrugged with one shoulder. "You can't leave until you know if I've accepted your apology or not." Julie walked away, heading down a narrow hallway and out of sight.

Well, hell. She'd made sure he couldn't leave now. He checked out her tidy little kitchen. There was a red vintage Formica-topped table and matching vinyl-padded chairs. The painted kitchen cupboards had shiny chrome pulls. There was a black-and-white checkerboard floor, and ruffled curtains in the window.

Julie's style was always so composed and conservative at work, but her house showed a playful side. He wasn't surprised to see that it was shiny clean— even the hardwood floors in the living room were gleaming. He walked in there and looked around. There weren't a lot of knickknacks—a few paintings and framed photos on the wall, but nothing sitting on the end tables or on the floor. Quinn smiled to himself. If she ever saw the "comfortable clutter" in his home, with Katie's schoolwork and his golf magazines everywhere, she'd probably break out in hives. And all the little nonsensical things that Anne used to collect on their trips when he was on tour. A cowboy figurine from Texas. A giant conch shell from San Diego. A snow globe from Wisconsin with two snowmen inside clinking together their mugs of beer. And all the family photos. He'd moved to Gallant Lake for a fresh start, but everywhere he looked in his house was a memory.

Julie's house, with all its *That '70s Show* kitsch, didn't give him the sense of things holding special memories for her. There was an assortment of framed photographs on the fireplace mantel, but oddly enough, Quinn *knew* everyone in them. Blake and Amanda. Nick and Cassie. Nora from the coffee shop and her furniture-building husband, Asher. Shane and Mel Brannigan.

But there were no childhood photos of Julie. No graduation photo. No photos of her with a boyfriend or anyone who looked like her parents. She had a big circle of friends here in Gallant Lake, but the display didn't tell him much about Julie herself. He picked up a small tourist souvenir—a faded plastic figure of a motorboat on water, with the words *Gallant Lake* at the base.

"I don't know why I keep that old thing." Julie walked into the room. To his relief—and a pinch of regret—she was in jeans and a baggy sweatshirt. Still beautiful and certainly looking more comfortable, but fully covered. "My mom gave it to me."

"That's a pretty good reason to keep it." Katie had shelves full of little touchstones reminding her of Anne.

Julie's eyes quickly cooled. "She picked it up off the ground near someone's trash can when I was ten and handed it to me. Then she said, 'Happy birthday, kid.'"

Quinn set the boat back on the mantel, trying to digest that short and devastating story. His own mom, living in Phoenix now, was about as close to sainthood as he could imagine any woman. Anne had been the same with Katie. Neither woman would dream of doing what Julie had described.

"That sounds, uh…" He had no idea what to say.

Julie flashed a quick, unconvincing smile. "It sounds pathetic. And it was. But I'm not looking for your pity." She looked at the plastic boat. "I guess I keep it to remind myself that I rose above that, despite everything. Coffee?"

The subject change was jarring, but he had a feeling she'd already shared more than she'd intended. There was a lot more going on inside composed, in-charge Julie Brown than he'd suspected. "Sure."

They went into the kitchen and she popped a pod into the coffee maker after asking his preference. He opted for decaf. His mornings started early at the golf course now that days were getting longer. She handed him a large mug, raising her brow when he added two heaping spoons of sugar. He shrugged with a smile.

"I know, the sugar rush probably defeats the idea of going decaf, but I'm a sucker for sweet things." He cringed at how that might sound, but Julie didn't pick up on the double meaning. She had no idea he considered *her* a sweet thing. His sudden surge of feelings after seeing her in that dress and touching her skin…well, that didn't mean anything other than Katie might be right about it being time for him to start dating. But with a coworker? No way in hell. Too messy.

Julie made herself a mug of coffee—full-strength and black, of course. No wonder she was like the Energizer Bunny at work. She was fully caffeinated 24/7. She pulled a foil cover off a plate and set it on the table as she joined him. The plate held an assortment of what looked like homemade cookies.

"Did you make these?" He selected a crescent-shaped cookie and groaned as he took a bite. "Whoa…that's really good."

"Cooking is my stress relief after dealing with people all day. Ingredients do what they're told." She took one of the chocolate cookies. Her comment made perfect sense to Quinn. Julie liked it when things went according to plan. Preferably *her* plan. She dunked the cookie in her coffee and took a bite, closing her eyes briefly in appreciation. "So…about that apology." Quinn blinked at the redirection but listened in silence as she continued. "I accept it, of course." A flush of color rose in her cheeks. "I was being a brat, and you were right to call me out on it. I'm sorry, too."

"We could keep saying 'No, *I'm* sorry' to each other all night," Quinn said. "Let's agree we both stepped over the line, we're both sorry and now we're back to behaving. But I do have a question for you."

She tipped her head to the side, waiting.

"Why are you *really* taking golf lessons? I mean, you don't like anything about golf, so…?"

She winced. "I don't know why I have so many opinions about the game." She took a sip of her coffee, staring at the darkness outside her kitchen window. Julie swallowed hard and shook her head before looking at him. "I guess I owe you the truth after you rescued me from that dress, but I swear to God if you tell anyone else, I'll *end* you."

That threat, which he didn't doubt was sincere, was more like what he expected from Julie. She was a take-no-prisoners sort when she wanted her way on something. He was way too curious not to give in to the demand. He held up one hand.

"I promise. I won't tell a soul."

She hesitated again. "I was trying to get a guy, okay? A guy who loves to golf. Amanda and Cassie gave him the impression that *I* golf, so I need to learn. Fast."

He thought he'd managed to tamp down his sudden attraction to Julie, but her words brought up a different emotion. One that felt an awful lot like jealousy.

I was trying to get a guy.

"What guy?" He knew it was none of his business. None of this was any of his business. But the question was out there now.

Her eyebrows gathered together. "I don't think that matters. He's new in town and he's a big golfer. My friends are determined to play matchmaker and I…" She grimaced. "And I let them. Probably because I'm afraid of growing old alone." He could barely hear the last words as her voice faded.

"You're not anywhere near *growing old*, Julie. You're young, smart, attractive and successful. I can't believe you have any problem finding dates."

"Well, thank you, but I'll be *forty* in a few months. That's not exactly young. And I'm—I'm not good at the whole dating thing. I haven't even been on a date in…" She laughed softly. "In years. And I have no clue why I'm telling *you* any of this."

It really was a mystery, Julie thought, the way being around Quinn just made her spill some of her most personal feelings. Telling him about that stupid plastic boat. Confessing the reason behind her golf lessons, then expanding on it by explaining how desperate she was not to become the town spinster.

Maybe it was the way he'd appeared at her door when she was trapped in the dress. How he'd handled all her suggestive begging about how he needed to help her out of that dress without being a creep about it.

Maybe it was the jolt of chemistry she'd felt when he was right behind her earlier, his fingers brushing her skin as he worked on the zipper. Or the way his words felt as he breathed them across the shockingly sensitive skin behind her ear.

She straightened in her chair. The fact that she'd reacted that strongly to *Quinn*, of all people, was proof that she needed to get out there and start dating. If not *Russ*…somebody. Even if it wasn't anything serious. Just…a man. For a night.

"Forty isn't exactly old, either." Quinn's voice was soft. *Oh, God—was he feeling sorry for her again?* "But I get what you're saying. Imagine how *I* feel. I'm forty-one and I've been off the dating market for decades. Katie thinks it's time, but I wouldn't even know where to start."

The air in the kitchen suddenly vibrated with some strange sort of tension. Quinn was leaning forward, and Julie realized she'd done the same. They were two people who'd just admitted to each other that they didn't know how to start dating. Maybe…

Nope. Not happening.

She sat back abruptly, and the movement made Quinn sit up, too. His cheeks took on a reddish hue.

He scrubbed the back of his neck. "That would have been a bad idea. Right?"

So he'd felt it, too. She nodded firmly.

"Very bad. You and me? No way. No offense, but…wow, such a bad idea. We can't get along at work, much less in…" She managed to stop before saying *bed*. Why on earth was she thinking of Quinn Walker and going to bed in the same breath?

He stood, still looking uncertain. And maybe a little rattled. "Right. We're coworkers. I should go. Um… I think we have another lesson scheduled for Friday, right?" He rushed on, talking faster as he went. "Now that I understand your goals, it gives me a better idea of what to focus on. You should pick up the basics pretty quickly, and then it's just lots of practice to improve muscle memory. As long as this guy you want to fool doesn't expect you to be too competitive, you'll be able to pull it off."

She followed him to the door, talking almost as fast as he was. "Great. Fantastic. And I promise to be more respectful of the game. It's your profession, after all, and the course brings a lot of business to the resort. Taking lessons might help me understand the attraction, right? Oh, and honestly…" He stopped and turned to listen after opening the door. "I do appreciate your making a special trip to apologize, and thank you for helping me with the broken zipper. That was above and beyond the call of duty for, you know…a coworker."

"Glad I could help." Quinn cleared his throat. "I'll see you Friday."

He was halfway down the sidewalk before Julie called from the door. "Quinn?" He turned. "You'll have no problem in the dating department, either. You'd be a catch."

He stared at the ground for a minute, then shook his head. "Thanks, but… I think it'll be a while before I get back in the game."

Of course. He'd lost his wife just a few years ago.

"If Katie is encouraging it, you should at least give it a try."

He grunted a laugh. "Katie thinks I'll die of loneliness once she heads off to college. If I'm dating, that lets her off the guilt-trip hook." He paused, giving Julie a wry grin. "But it's not her guilt I'm worried about. It would be…weird…to be with anyone but my wife."

But your wife is gone. Julie knew better than to say that out loud. Grieving could be a complicated process. "Then you should definitely take your time. There's no schedule for when to start dating again after…what you've been through." This was a heavy conversation to be having standing on the sidewalk. "I should get back inside. Thanks again for everything."

He said, "Good night" and walked away. When

she closed the door, the air inside her house still vibrated, as if there was an energy there that hadn't existed before. Quinn was gone, but the energy remained, making her skin tingle and keeping her awake much of the night.

Chapter Seven

"That's good," Quinn said, grinning at Julie. "Use the whole body in your swing, not just your arms. When you finish your swing, your hips should have rotated enough to face the direction your ball is going."

Julie stood with her club on her shoulder as she watched the golf ball sail out over the driving range, passing the hundred-yard marker in something close to the right direction. Her expression radiated pride, mixed with a little surprise. That was normal with a new golfer—the first time they put all the tips into practice successfully, they thought they had now figured out the game of golf.

Sure enough, she looked at him with a bright smile. "That felt amazing! It even sounded different, with that little ping sound. And look how far it went! It's almost like I'm a real golfer or something."

"Or something." Quinn held up his hands in defense when she scowled. "I'm not trying to burst your bubble, but you've had four lessons in two weeks. You're doing great, but this is when the real work begins."

Her face fell as she lowered the golf club. "*Real* work? What do you call what I've been doing?"

"You know *what* to do. The secret is to train your body to do that swing consistently. You hit the hell out of that driver, but you don't drive every shot on the course. Your short game is where you win or lose…" She was still staring in dismay, and he realized he wasn't exactly motivating her. One thing he'd learned about Julie was she responded better to positive feedback than negative. He took a breath and started over. "That swing was fantastic, Julie. You've come a long way in two weeks—faster than most of my students. I'm definitely impressed."

Her whole body relaxed at his praise, and her smile returned. It wasn't that she craved empty praise—in fact, she'd call him out on it if she thought he was patronizing her. But she definitely did *not* like negative feedback. She didn't argue with it or get defensive, but her body language was clear. It hit her hard. Someone else might not notice, but

Quinn had begun cataloging everything about the woman. When she heard something that might be taken as a critique, she absorbed it like a blow. He'd done his best to adjust how he instructed her, but teaching involved correcting. He stepped closer to her, waiting until her eyes met his.

"Hey, you are right where you should be. In fact, you're ahead of the curve. I know how hard you push yourself, and I don't want you to get frustrated."

And there it was, that slight easing in her facial expression and the set of her shoulders. She tipped her head to the side. "You know how hard I push myself? That's a pretty personal observation for someone who barely knows me. Should I be worried?"

They were back to their comfort zone—snarking on each other. "It's my job as an instructor to read my students' body language and figure out their learning style. But even before you started lessons, I knew you were driven. You're always on the go at the resort, making sure every little detail is taken care of."

"That's *my* job."

"Yes, but you take that responsibility more seriously than some might. Take, for example, the way you thought you had the best ideas for the golf tournament." He winked to let her know he was teasing. "And I've seen that spotless house of yours. And you told me you like to cook because ingredients *behave*, which is a pretty good indicator of someone who likes things to be under her control."

She considered his words, then nodded with a rueful smile. "You really *have* been paying attention. It's not the first time someone's suggested I'm a control freak. I like having plans. I do *not* like surprises, especially at work. And when I take on a new hobby or goal, I *do* take it seriously." She hesitated. "Maybe more seriously than I should."

He took the golf club from her and they walked back to the pro shop together. There was something between them that made both of them open up about things.

"What do you do for fun, Julie?"

She looked up in surprise. "Lots of things. Why?"

"You said you don't like surprises. I think of having fun as being open to something spontaneous and unexpected. You know—an impromptu cookout with friends, maybe a spin around the lake on the boat, or Katie chasing me around the house with a glass of cold water for a game of tag. Those are fun to me. What's fun to you?"

He held open the door and she went past him into the shop. She was laughing.

"Why would Katie chase you with a water glass *indoors*? She doesn't actually...?"

"Throw water on me? Damn right she does, if she can get close enough. I know how to get my revenge, though. Sometimes her wake-up call is a cold drizzle of water on her face."

She looked horrified. "In the *house*? You throw water on each other in the *house*." She shook her head in amazement. "And you think that's *fun*? Who cleans it up afterward? What if it gets on the wall? Or on her bed?"

Quinn set the bag of clubs down near the counter. "It's *water*, not fruit punch. It's not going to stain anything, although we try to avoid the leather sectional. Whoever ends up the wettest has to dry everything with a towel."

"That would most definitely *not* be fun for me. I like to ride my bike on the back roads or hike up Gallant Mountain. I enjoy reading. I ski in the winter. Those things are fun." She brightened. "And, of course, I hang out with my friends—that's fun, too."

"Until they set you up with some stranger and make you learn how to golf."

She laughed. "Well, there is that." Her smile faded. "But learning to golf isn't all bad."

Quinn couldn't argue there. He looked forward to their lessons. Like today, they often ended up talking about what was going on in their lives. Which reminded him—

"Hey, I forgot to ask...when's the wedding?"

Julie took a step back, her eyes open wide. "Excuse me? I haven't even golfed with the guy yet!"

"I wasn't talking about Russ. I meant the wedding you're wearing that pink dress to."

Julie put her hand on her hip. "First, I don't remember telling you the guy's name was Russ. Second, I wore that dress in a wedding ten years ago."

Quinn kicked himself for saying Russ's name. He handed her a sports drink from the cooler behind the counter. "First, you said it was a new, single guy who loves golf. The only new golfer I know in town is Russ Gantry. And second, why were you trying on a ten-year-old bridesmaid gown?"

"First…" Julie held up her hand, then waved it back and forth to erase the word. "Forget the counting. Yes, it's Russ I'm learning to golf for. He's good-looking and nice and seems…interested. He told me he'd like to have coffee sometime. And I was trying on the dress for charity. I'm donating my closet full of bridesmaid dresses to the fashion show we have for the Travis Foundation weekend. Mel Brannigan and her designer friend, Luis, are doing a challenge to repurpose or update the dresses."

"You have a *closet* full of bridesmaid dresses? How many times have you been a bridesmaid?"

Her cheeks took on a tinge of pink. She had a wide range of blushes, but this was his favorite—just a slight touch of soft color high on her cheeks.

"Let's just say too many." She scrunched her nose. "That's why I'm trying to figure out how to date properly, because clearly I've been doing it wrong all these years."

They walked out into the clubhouse dining area, where two older guys were drinking coffee near the window. Steve and John were regulars at the course and liked to get their golf in early before relaxing at a table by the window for an hour or so. Often, like today, they had a cribbage board between them. Quinn waved a greeting and gestured toward a table in the corner for Julie to sit at.

"So you think you've been doing it wrong just because you're not married?"

Julie turned her drink bottle on the table back and forth a few times. "Well, the whole bridesmaid fourteen times and bride none sends a certain message, don't you think?"

He raised one shoulder. "Maybe it means you haven't met the right guy yet. But I gotta be honest…" He gave her a pointed look. "Finding a spouse isn't something you can solve with spreadsheets and timetables. Instead of secretly taking golf lessons to fool Russ, maybe you should try being honest. He might surprise you." Quinn managed to hold back his smile. He was very sure Russ would surprise Julie once she made her designs on him known. "Falling in love is one of those things that just happens, Julie. Out of the blue, you meet someone and your heart does a flip-flop for no discernable reason at all, and boom. You're in love."

Her eyes narrowed, so he told a story he hadn't shared in a while. "For example, Anne and I literally ran in to each other at the grocery store late one night. She came rushing around the corner and banged her cart into mine, sending my tower of frozen dinners tumbling down over the beer and bags of chips in the bottom of my cart. She apologized, then told me my grocery choices were terrible. That was the start of our romance." He'd looked at Anne's cart, full of fresh produce, seafood, spices and other mysteries, and told Anne he would have no idea what to do with all that. She offered to teach him and invited him over for dinner the next night. They were married six months later, and pregnant with Katie three months after that. The happiest days of his life.

"Maybe I should hang out in the grocery store more often to look for a date." Julie took a sip of her drink. "That's where Nora and Asher Peyton met, too."

"You missed the point," Quinn answered. "If you're there 'looking for a date,' then it's not spontaneous."

"I think you know by now that I don't *do* spontaneous well."

"Maybe you need a little practice. After all, practice is what makes you a better golfer, so it might help get your dating muscles back in shape, too."

Julie's right eyebrow arched high. "Are you offering to be my *dating* instructor as well as my golfing instructor?"

That wasn't at all what Quinn had intended, but it didn't sound like such a bad idea. *They* might be a bad idea for any sort of genuine relationship, but surely he could teach her a thing or two about dating. He'd done enough of it before meeting Anne, and he'd managed to convince *her* to marry him, so he had skills to offer.

"I was referring more to being spontaneous than actual dating, but…sure. I'd be happy to answer any questions from a guy's perspective. And we could work on that spontaneity thing, too."

Julie's lips pursed, forming a near kiss shape, which was very distracting. Quinn had to think about doing inventory again to calm his libido.

"I can do without the spontaneity, but I could use the dating feedback." Her eyes narrowed on him. "What do *you* get out of this deal? Because I am not paying you money to be my dating guru."

He held up his hands. "I don't want you to pay me. That would be…creepy. But I'm happy to help, as a friend."

"So we're friends now?"

"I've unzipped you out of a dress in your house, so I guess we could be friends." The thought of his fingers on her skin was enough to force him to repeat the word *inventory* over and over in his mind. They might have come close to crossing the line that night, but they'd both managed to step back in the nick of time.

The brush of pink in her cheeks deepened. "Fair enough. But what if we exchange favors?"

His brain filled with enticing, but unlikely, possibilities. "What did you have in mind?"

"You admitted your dating skills were rusty, too. Why don't we help each other? You give *me* feedback, and I'll give *you* feedback." He was about to object, but she talked over him. "I know you don't think you're ready, and that's fine. But when you *are* ready, you'll know what to do. I realize you're Mr. Spontaneous, but you also lecture me about *muscle memory* all the time, so think of it as building your muscle memory for dating."

He had no idea how this was going to play out, but after preaching about being open to new things, he didn't feel like he could protest. "Fair enough. We'll exchange advice and get feedback from each other."

"Right. But this isn't a fake-dating thing. We're not going out with each other. We've already established we're a bad idea." She said it so matter-of-factly that he wondered if she remembered how intense that moment was in her kitchen. She was all business now, sitting up and clearly embracing the plan. The woman loved a plan. "This will be strictly an…information exchange, with a little practice when needed. Maybe some roleplay of certain situations." She looked at him with a firm gaze. "Of nonphysical situations. No touching."

The fact that she felt the need to emphasize that told him she *did* remember that moment in her house and the energy that had bounced around the room like a ricocheting bullet.

After Julie headed off to the resort, Quinn couldn't stop wondering how this was going to work. He'd be helping her land another man. He was pretty sure it wouldn't be Russ Gantry, but there were plenty of guys in Gallant Lake who'd consider themselves worthy of her. That was a good thing, since Quinn wasn't interested. The little sparks of sexual chemistry between them were just the revving of an engine that hadn't quite started yet. He wasn't sure if he'd *ever* be ready for someone new.

So why did the idea of helping Julie find her Mr. Right feel so very wrong?

"Hey, Katie, did you check on…?" Julie scrolled through her on-screen planner, but there was no need.

"On the corner suite for Mr. and Mrs. Carthage?" Katie reached behind her head to tug her ponytail tighter. "It's all set. Strictly one-hundred-percent cotton sheets and towels washed in scent-free detergent. Down pillows—no fake foam or fiber to be seen. There's nothing but organic, fair-trade, dark-roast coffee pods with the coffee maker. Oh, and I removed the mattress from the bed and replaced it with a horsehair pad on the floor for them to sleep on."

Julie gave a startled laugh. "What?"

Katie grinned. "Well, I figured if they're so determined to go back to nature in their five-hundred-dollar-a-night luxury suite, then they wouldn't want to sleep on a foam mattress, right?"

Leave it to a teenager to call out hypocrisy. The girl was sharper than her dad. Not *smarter.* But sharper in her approach to things. Sharper-tongued. Sharper-eyed. She'd lost her mom at fourteen, after watching her deal with cancer for two years before that. Julie first heard the story from Amanda, and then from Katie herself last summer, when she was working part-time at the resort. She said she was able to talk about it because her father had insisted they go to counseling together *and* individually. It was no surprise the teen intended to study psychology in college.

"Very funny, Katie. As you know—"

"Yes, yes," she answered. "The Carthages are very good clients of the resort and have already booked their daughter's wedding for next year so we need to keep them happy."

"Actually, we need to keep—"

"We need to keep *all* of our clients happy. I *know.* Don't worry, the mattress in their room is still intact and they can have happy little hypocritical dreams on it."

Katie checked her phone discreetly behind the counter, making sure no guest would see her. That was a firm rule of Julie's—no cell phones, or at least no cell phones for more than ten seconds, and never where a guest could see. She couldn't completely defeat the technology of the twenty-first century, but she could damn sure control it. Katie slid the phone back into her pocket with a heavy sigh.

"Everything okay?" Julie asked.

"Yeah, it's my dad letting me know he's grilling steak for dinner and asking if I want green beans or grilled summer squash as a side." Katie sounded annoyed, which made Julie laugh.

"Wow, what a jerk. I'm so sorry he's putting you through that."

Katie joined in the laughter. "I know, right? I just wish he'd get a life other than taking care of me. I'll be gone in August. He needs to get out there and find somebody fast."

"Honey, your dad will be okay. He'll miss you, but he'll be fine. He has his job and he has friends, and you'll be back to visit."

Katie looked panicked. "He needs someone to come home to, Julie. That's why I keep trying to get him to start dating." She brightened. "Hey, you're taking lessons now. Maybe you and he—"

"Forget it." Julie held her hand up to stop her. "Your dad and I are coworkers. Workplace romances are messy. And besides, I don't feel that way about your father." Funny how she hadn't led with that.

Katie wasn't convinced. "Didn't Nick and Cassie meet working here and fall in love? Now they're married!"

"Apparently you missed the part where I said I don't feel that way about your dad. If you're worried about him being lonely, buy him a cat. Heck, I've got one he can have." She wouldn't really give up Fluff, of course. The cranky feline had made herself at home with Julie.

"It's not just that." Katie looked around. The reception desk was quiet and the afternoon shift was arriving. Katie's voice dropped. "Can I tell you a secret?"

"Uh…sure. Of course."

"I promised my mom I'd help Dad find someone new, and I haven't done it."

From everything Julie had heard about Quinn's late wife, pressuring her young daughter to become a matchmaker didn't fit the image at all. Julie led Katie back to the small staff room, where they could have some privacy. They sat at the break table. Katie's eyes were shining with unshed tears, and Julie reached for her hand.

"What exactly did your mom ask you to do?"

"It was a couple months before she died. Dad had driven us to the beach. Mom and I got settled in our beach chairs under the umbrella, and Dad went walking near the water to find Mom some seashells. She used to love going shelling, but she wasn't up to it anymore." Katie stared straight ahead, replaying the moment. "We talked about a lot of grown-up stuff those last few months. I think she was trying to cram a lifetime of mothering into the time she had left. She talked about dating and stuff. I had a crush on a cute boy in the neighborhood, but he'd said something mean to me. Mom told me that any boy who made me cry wasn't worth crying over."

"That's pretty good advice," Julie said. She wondered if it applied to parents who made you cry.

"Yeah, it is." Katie smiled, and the tears didn't seem to be threatening anymore. "We watched Dad picking up shells and tossing a starfish back into the ocean. That's when Mom told me that Dad should find someone new to love after she was gone. I argued, but she shut me down. She told me that she *wanted* it to happen, that she wanted him to find happiness again, and that I needed to accept that it was going to happen someday. Not only accept it, but she said I should *help* Dad find someone who made him happy. Or at least stay out of the way if it happened. I promised I would. But I haven't done it. I didn't want to share him. I definitely didn't want—" she made air quotes with her fingers "—a 'new mom.' I mean, what if I hated her? Things were good with only him and me, you know? But… I *promised*. And now I'm leaving for school…"

Her voice faded off and they sat in silence for a moment. Julie couldn't help thinking, once again, what a clever and caring young woman Quinn and his late wife had raised. But right now she was carrying far too much responsibility on those shoulders. Julie might not be a mom, but she was *Auntie Julie* to Amanda's kids, along with all the new babies coming along among her friends. Surely she could come up with some sage advice here.

"You were fourteen at the time?" Katie nodded, sniffling and reaching for a tissue. "I understand you may have used the words *I promise*, but honey, it doesn't sound like your mom exactly asked you to be your father's matchmaker. She asked you not to intervene, and to accept that he might *someday* want to fall in love again. You haven't broken that promise. Quinn isn't ready…" Katie looked up in surprise that Julie would know that, and she tried to clarify without betraying what he'd told her. "What I mean is, I think if he *was* ready, he'd be out there dating, right? There's plenty of time for him to meet someone and fall in love again. Love isn't something you can schedule. It just sort of happens when least expected."

She tried not to smile at the irony of repeating Quinn's words—ones she'd *argued* with—to his own daughter. "Maybe your going off to school will motivate him to start thinking about it, but it doesn't need to happen *before* you go."

Katie thought about that, then nodded. "I guess

you're right. Mom and Dad met when they literally bumped into each other in the grocery store, so it can happen anytime."

"I know." *Dammit!* She kept sharing more than she intended, and Katie picked up on it.

"You know how they met? Did Dad tell you?"

"What? Oh… I meant I know love can happen anytime. That's a cute story, though." She remembered the warmth in Quinn's eyes as he'd shared it while sipping coffee at her kitchen table.

"Oh, right. Dad hardly ever talks about Mom except with me. He doesn't like talking about her with people who didn't know her. Those memories belong to him and me, you know?"

Julie nodded, but she couldn't help thinking that he didn't seem at all uncomfortable talking about Anne that night. He hadn't been tense or sad or awkward. He was the one who'd brought her up. Right after his fingers had lingered against Julie's back. *Oh, God.* Had that moment been nothing more than a trigger of memories of his late wife?

If so, then Quinn was right—he definitely wasn't ready to start dating. And the two of them together, even briefly, would be a truly terrible idea. He wouldn't be with her at all. He'd be touching her but remembering another woman.

Chapter Eight

"We're actually going to *golf* today? On the course?" Julie stared at Quinn with a mix of surprise and anticipation. "You think I'm ready?"

She was so eager, charging ahead all the time, wanting to be the best.

"For a tournament? No. For a casual round of golf?" He paused for dramatic effect. "Also, no." She stuck her tongue out at him. "The point is we'll never know if we don't get out there." He gestured toward the waiting golf cart.

"But… I wasn't ready. Am I dressed right? Do I have everything I need?"

"Ah, yes. I forgot you couldn't handle surprises." He secured the bags to the cart and once again gestured for her to get in. "Consider this two lessons in one. How to be spontaneous and how to play golf on an actual golf course."

She muttered a few curse words, but she got into the cart and gamely said, "Let's do this."

It was a beautiful morning for golf. The sun was bright on the mountains, and the lake was like glass. There was the promise of summer warmth in the air. As far as the golf went, she did well for her first time. She whiffed on a few balls, missing them completely with the golf club. She hit the ground a few times, making her grimace as the impact resonated up her arms. But when she *did* connect with the ball, she sent it in relatively the right direction, and got a fair bit of distance out of it. By August, she'd be ready to impress Russ at the charity tournament. And hopefully some other guy, too, because Russ would be golfing that day with his new boyfriend, Elliot. A little detail the fastidious Julie had missed.

Quinn leaned against the cart on the fifth fairway and watched as Julie hacked away at the ball. She was running out of steam. She'd had a good drive here but had worked herself into a state after missing the ball twice with the iron, then clipping the top of the ball so it barely bounced three feet.

"Okay," Quinn said. "Step back and take a breath before you wear yourself out. You're trying too hard."

She flashed him a dark look. "There's no such thing as trying too hard. I'm not quitting."

"I didn't say you should quit. Just take a break and relax. Golf is one of those games where the harder you try, the worse you do." He took the club from her hand. "It's a golf club, not a machete."

He set the club against the cart, then took both of her hands by the fingertips and gently shook her arms to loosen her up. "Roll your shoulders. Shake off your foul mood and try to enjoy yourself."

"But I suck!" But she rolled her shoulders and neck, closing her eyes.

"You don't suck. You're *learning.* Anytime you learn something new, you go through a sucky phase, but it won't last." He ran his hands up and down her arms, doing his best to ignore the jolt of electricity it caused somewhere in his chest. "Look around. You're outside in the fresh air. The birds are singing. The view is incredible." This was the course's signature hole, running along the shore of Gallant Lake. The surrounding mountains were shades of vibrant green.

But Quinn wasn't looking at the mountains. He was looking at Julie Brown. Her bright yellow golf visor brought out the golden highlights in her hair, which was pulled back in a low ponytail. Her eyes were still closed, her long lashes lying against her soft skin. Her lips parted slightly, and he noticed for the first time that they were the color of the dark pink roses starting to blossom along the side of the clubhouse. He wasn't rubbing her arms anymore. His hands had come to rest on her shoulders.

Her eyes swept open without warning, and their gazes locked. They both froze.

Think about doing inventory. Kissing her is a bad idea.

He released her and coughed a few times, trying to gather his wits back about him.

"What I was trying to say was…this isn't a game you can play if you're tensed up."

"Which game are you referring to, exactly?"

The question was provocative, and Quinn couldn't help chuckling in response.

"Both of them—golf and dating. And being spontaneous, for that matter. All three require the ability to relax and go with the flow." He handed her the golf club. "They also require the proper time and place. Right now, right here is the proper time and place for *golf.* Let's finish this hole and call it quits for today."

"Why can't we stop right now?"

"Nuh-uh. No way are you stopping before hitting that golf ball, lazy bones. We'll stay here until you get it right…"

He was teasing, of course. But Julie almost recoiled at the words—not physically, but in some small way that he was able to pick up on. Quinn recognized the stricken look in her eyes from that first, disastrous lesson, when she'd fled after he'd criticized her. He reached for her, but she jerked away, walking to her golf ball.

Neither of them said a word as she took her position and swung the club with lethal force. The ball flew forward, landing near the edge of the green. She put the club in her bag and got in the cart alongside him, staring ahead in silence. He pressed the accelerator, shaking his head.

"If picturing my face on the golf ball made you hit it that far, feel free to do that from now on."

The corners of her mouth curled in as she fought her answering smile. She tipped back her head and sighed, shaking off whatever had irritated her. She finally gave him a sideways look. "It wasn't you I was picturing."

His careless words had made her angry. Who else would she be picturing as she whipped that golf club through the air? They picked up their golf balls instead of finishing. That powerful hit had been her best of the day, and perfect to end on. But Quinn didn't drive back to the clubhouse. He didn't have any lessons scheduled until later that afternoon, and Jerry was covering the pro shop. And he had some questions for his current student.

"Where are we going?"

Julie wanted nothing more than to get back home and away from this man who had the uncanny ability to push all her buttons. She never let random comments from people fire her up. But let Quinn say *anything* that could possibly be taken as a criticism, and she found herself feeling like a lanky, uncertain teenager who never heard anything *but* criticism. Why did his words have more power over her than anyone else's did?

Quinn drove the golf cart through an opening in the trees that led toward the lake. The golf course vanished, and the shoreline stretched toward the mountains. To the right she could see the resort, and the towers of Blake and Amanda's historic castle, Halcyon, beyond that. To the left were the new vacation townhomes and the town of Gallant Lake. This spot, where Quinn had now stopped, felt private and insulated from the rest of the world. He shifted in his seat to face her.

"The golf lesson is over, but it feels like time for a lesson in being spontaneous."

"So you decided to kidnap me to a secluded location?"

He chuckled, but quickly grew serious. "It's one of my favorite thinking spots, but if you're not comfortable—"

"I was kidding. I'm fine." She looked around. "It's peaceful here."

"*Are* you fine, though?"

"Excuse me?" Julie straightened, feeling that familiar tension Quinn tended to ignite in her.

He sighed. "Look, I may not always pick the best words, especially around you, but I don't understand what happens when I say something that bothers you. I don't even know *why* it bothers you when it happens." His hand was on the back of the seat, and when he shifted his weight again, his fingers brushed her shoulder. "That first lesson when you stormed off, and then today. Am I wrong about...?"

Julie shook her head. Not only did he push her buttons, but he was also intensely perceptive. "No, you're not wrong. Sometimes I'm extra sensitive to negative comments." She stared out over the water. "I can't explain it."

She *could* explain it. She just didn't want to. She didn't want to think about her childhood creeping back into her life after she'd finally put it behind her.

"Think that will be a deal-breaker for my dating life?"

He gave her a soft smile. "Knowing you have a problem is the first step to fixing it, right? Don't let some guy's comments rattle you, especially mine. You know who you are, and you don't need to worry about other people's opinions so much."

She looked away. "Easier said than done."

Especially when it seemed to be only *his* opinions that affected her so sharply.

"I know," he agreed. "But you shouldn't give any guy that kind of power over you." His fingers moved back and forth on her shoulder. "Who are you hearing when the words hit that way? It seems I'm triggering something or someone from the past."

She huffed out a laugh. "Triggering? Did you learn that word in counseling? Very astute observation, Dr. Walker."

Now it was his turn to recoil. He sat back with a frown, his eyebrows lowering. "Who told you that? Katie?" He shook his head. "Little Miss Share My Life With Everyone. It was only for six months or so after we moved here. Katie was struggling, and I was doing everything wrong, so we went to family counseling and the counselor wanted us to do some individual sessions—"

Julie reached out, putting her hand on his arm. "You don't need to defend yourself, Quinn. There's nothing wrong with getting help."

He didn't answer right away. "I didn't mean to sound like mental health care is anything to be ashamed of. I'm more private than my daughter when it comes to that stuff. We had a problem. We dealt with it. We moved on."

She huffed out a laugh. "That is such a man thing to say."

Quinn chuckled. "Yeah, I guess it is. Must be that fragile ego of ours." He arched an eyebrow at her. "And you still haven't answered my question. Who are you hearing whenever I come close to saying something negative?"

She squinted out at the water. He was the only

one pushing that particular button, so she might as well tell him. "Let's just say I didn't get a lot of positive feedback as a kid. In fact, I didn't get *any* positive feedback. Just lots and lots of insults. I thought I'd worked through it, but thinking about getting into a serious relationship has it bubbling up again." She looked at Quinn, getting lost in his dark eyes, before she blinked away her reverie. "Makes sense, since that's what's stopped me from getting serious all this time. I've been told I have trust issues. I guess I'll have to get over that before I try to ask Russ Gantry on a date, huh?"

Quinn grimaced, glancing away.

"What?"

"About Russ…" He blew out a long breath as his words trailed off.

"Oh, my God." She grinned. "He doesn't really like golf after all? He collects toenail clippings? He's a serial killer? Tell me!"

"He's got a boyfriend." Quinn winced again. "A man friend, or whatever. He's a great guy, and so is his partner, Elliot. But if Russ suggested a round of golf and coffee with you, that's *all* he wanted. Sorry."

Julie fell back against the seat. "Of course. I can't even *pick* the right guy, much less worry about keeping him. I'm going to be a bridesmaid forever." Her frustration propelled her out of the cart and walking down the lakeshore. Quinn scrambled to follow her.

"I don't believe that for one minute. You once said I'd be a catch. Well, you would, too. You're attractive and smart and funny."

She wanted to believe it, but kept getting hung up on his word choices for some reason. *Attractive* felt too close to *adequate*. "Well...thanks for the glowing review, but maybe I should embrace my spinster future. I already have the cat."

"Julie..." Quinn waited until she stopped and looked up at him. "There is no way you should be alone for the rest of your life." His voice was low and surprisingly intense. "I wasn't kidding—any man would be lucky to have you. Stop believing whatever people told you in the past. You're successful and beautiful and you deserve to have someone in your life."

The corners of her mouth rose. "*Beautiful* sounds better than *attractive*. But I think I missed my window of opportunity, Quinn. I was too busy making a career and getting my degree and just...doing everything but dating. And I have a good life—"

"If you believed that, you wouldn't have signed up for golf lessons just for a chance to go on a date with some guy you didn't know."

She grimaced. "That was an impulse move, spurred on by my well-meaning friends and all those bridesmaid dresses. I had a burst of self-pity but it's over now. Forget about golf. Forget about Russ. I'm better off alone anyway."

"Speaking of self-pity…"

"Yeah, that sounded bad. But maybe I'm not cut out for putting my heart in someone else's hands. Looks like you're off the hook with all the lessons— for golf *and* dating."

She turned back toward the golf cart, but he took her arm and stopped her. He moved in front of her, his eyes never leaving hers. "If you want to quit golf lessons, fine, but I'll miss them. If you want to quit the dating game, that's your choice, even if I disagree."

Their chests were nearly touching. His hands were on her shoulders, slowly sliding toward the base of her neck. His face was just above hers now, so close she could see the shards of ebony in his dark brown eyes, like a glimpse of the night sky. His voice was a whisper, blowing soft on her cheek.

"But I don't think you should stop trying to live in the moment." His thumbs now brushed the sensitive skin behind her ears, where she could hear her own blood swooshing through her veins. "What do you say, Julie? Ready to do something spontaneous?"

What was happening?

"Are you planning on kissing me?"

Humor shone in his eyes. "I hadn't planned on it when the day started, but right now it feels like something I definitely want to do." His head dipped lower, his lips so close to hers that she felt their magnetic pull. "But only if you want me to."

Yes, please! Then a sobering thought whispered to her doubts.

"Is this a pity kiss? Because if it is—"

He hushed whatever it was she was going to say—because seriously, how could she be expected to remember?—when his mouth covered hers. His lips were firm and his kiss was self-assured. Commanding without being arrogant. Skilled. She moaned and sagged into his embrace. *Definitely* skilled.

His tongue knew exactly what to do, and she didn't hesitate to give in, parting her lips and rising up on her toes to give him easier access to her mouth. To everything. One of his hands cupped the back of her head. The other cupped her bottom, holding her close enough to feel his response. She moved her hips and he growled against her mouth, muttering a curse before plunging back into her with his tongue.

Julie slid her hands behind his head, holding his mouth on hers. Electricity surged through her body and she didn't want to lose its source. This kiss could last forever as far as she was concerned. This kiss with Quinn Walker. The golf pro. Her coworker. The grieving widower who'd called them a bad idea. A chill swept over her and, even though she didn't move from his embrace, her desire began to cool.

He noticed the change in her—he had an uncanny way of reading her. His mouth slid off hers and he trailed lighter kisses down her jaw and below her ear. His breathing was labored as he pressed his face into her neck.

"For the record," he began, his voice filled with gravel, "that was *not* a pity kiss. It was an in-the-moment kiss that managed to shock even me. Holy hell, Julie." He raised his head, still holding her close, his arms linked at the small of her back. Hers were wrapped around his neck. She shook her head.

"*That* was something we agreed would be a very bad idea, Mr. Spontaneous."

Chapter Nine

Even the thought of doing all-day inventories every day for the rest of his life couldn't calm Quinn's body right now. He was still hard and ready, hotly pressed against Julie's body. But…this was *Julie*. She was looking for husband material. And that most definitely was *not* him. He lifted his head and stared down into her golden eyes, her pupils dilating so much they were like shining mirrors. He recognized the fire he saw there, but he also knew that nothing good could come from it. Not with her.

"It sure didn't *feel* like a bad idea, but you're right. It was…" He was going to say *a mistake*, but the words refused to come. And rightly so. Calling that rock-star kiss anything close to a mistake would be a grave injustice. "It was wonderful." Her eyes softened in relief and he thanked himself for catching the other words in time. He brushed her cheek with his fingers. "That was one stellar kiss. Breathtaking. Perfect."

Julie scoffed, rolling her eyes. "Okay, okay. You don't have to lay it on *that* thick."

His fingers gripped her chin, and her eyes went wide when his voice hardened. "Don't do that. Don't do the deprecating thing you do where you act like you can't possibly deserve to be as terrific as you are." He kissed her again. He couldn't help himself.

This time it was slower. Softer. Her lips parted and he accepted the invitation, but with more restraint. More appreciation of where he was and who he was with. Their breathing was in sync. His hand slid down to rest on her chest. Their heartbeats were in sync as well. He hadn't felt anything like this since…

He stepped back abruptly, leaving Julie teetering from losing his support, blinking in surprise. He took her arm, but resisted pulling her any closer.

"You really are something, but I can't… I haven't… Not since—"

"Oh, God, Quinn. Was that your first kiss since you lost your wife?" She covered her face with her hands. "I'm sorry…"

"Don't be sorry. Please." He waited until she lowered her hands enough to look at him. Her cheeks were flaming. "I don't regret it, and I sure don't want *you* to regret it. But I need to figure out what this means. To my marriage." He gave a mirthless laugh. This confession was going to make him sound crazy. "I know my wife is dead, but I still haven't wrapped my head around not being married, if that makes any sense—"

"That makes perfect sense to me." Julie smiled softly, and he could see that mantle of practical efficiency settling back over her shoulders. "Let's just, maybe not *forget*, but…*set aside* this morning as an interesting detour."

"Okay." He knew those kisses would be impossible to forget. "We could call it…practicing. You know, making sure you're ready to date." His face felt hot at the thought of her kissing anyone else. "A little role play. You, uh, did very well."

She arched an eyebrow. "Are you saying we were working on developing muscle memory?"

He chuckled. "Exactly. Good news—we both remember how to do it."

"Thanks, coach."

"But if you feel a need to *practice* some more, I'm available."

"I thought you just said—"

"I know. You're right. But we have something, Julie. At your place. Here today." Their chemistry was undeniable. "Maybe we should explore this detour…?"

"Maybe we shouldn't." Her voice was emphatic.

He wasn't going to push it. She was probably right, no matter how disappointing it was. He cleared his throat. "Of course. Right. I should get back to work. I wouldn't want you reporting to Blake that I was slacking off during working hours."

Julie laughed and fell in at his side as he walked to the cart. "I think we can agree that our employer doesn't need to know *anything* about this particular lesson. Or anyone else, for that matter."

"Very definitely agreed."

But he'd sure as hell never forget it.

When Friday morning dawned drizzly and cool, Quinn wondered if Julie would show up for her lesson. They hadn't confirmed anything after their *detour* on Monday, and technically she'd said she was done with golf when she discovered Russ *was* a devoted golfer, but was *not* husband material. At least not for her. Nine o'clock passed and he figured she really had quit. That stung more than he expected, and he was going to miss their sharp-edged conversations that so often turned personal. And just that once had turned intimate. He went into the pro shop and started unboxing and steaming the new shirts that had arrived yesterday.

He was still getting over his guilt about kissing Julie. They'd been two consenting, single adults, of course. But Quinn really hadn't considered himself single before then. He damn sure knew he was alone. He understood that Anne was gone forever. But he'd thrown himself so deeply into raising Katie the best he could that he hadn't taken much time to grapple with his marriage ending the day Anne died. He'd worked through his grief over her death with the family counselor, but he'd never specifically grieved the loss of his marriage.

In his heart, he still felt married to the woman who'd made him laugh and encouraged him to stick to the golf tour as a career when his parents and friends were suggesting he find a Plan B. She'd been his partner and career adviser as much as his lover, best friend and mother of his child. He'd been one of the lucky ones to have a love like that. Only a fool would think he'd have more than one chance for that. And he was no fool.

He started putting the colorful shirts on a rack in the center of the store. There was a corporate tournament coming up tomorrow. Later today he'd put the goody bags together for the players, with a hat from the club and a water bottle with the company's logo on it, along with an assortment of energy bars and a sleeve of golf balls.

"Nice product placement."

He looked up in surprise. Julie was in the doorway, smiling as if nothing awkward had ever happened between them. She was in a bright green golf skirt and a yellow top. Her legs were long and tan. He cleared his throat. He needed to keep his eyes off her legs. He started hanging more shirts.

"These just came in yesterday afternoon. I figured I'd put them front and center for the tourney tomorrow." He glanced at the clock on the wall. It was a promo display from a manufacturer, with a golf ball as the clock face and golf clubs for hands. "I thought you were blowing off the lesson. It's pretty wet out there."

"I didn't think there was any hurry, considering the weather." She walked over to the wall where he had the womens' golf clothing on display and moved a few hangers to examine the shirts. "There's a wicked stomach flu going around, and I had to juggle weekend schedules a bit."

He nodded. "Katie said some of her friends had it this week. From what I hear, it's fast but nasty." He put the last of the shirts on the rack. "If it was next week, I could offer you an indoor lesson, but the new driving booth radar system isn't set up yet."

"Why don't you teach me more about what you do when you're not golfing?" She looked at the wall of clothing. "How do you know what to order for the shop? What do you have to do to run a tournament?"

He put his hand on his hip. "Are you looking to steal my job?"

She chuckled. "Hardly. But it couldn't hurt for us to learn a bit about each other's jobs, even if it's just to avoid being called into the boss's office to settle arguments." She flashed a playful grin, nodding toward where John and Steve were already setting up their cribbage board by the window. "And it keeps us away from any tempting detours, since there will be people around."

The so-called lesson stretched on longer than an hour, but by the end of it, Julie knew the basic setup of the pro shop and office, as well as the software he used to keep track of players' handicaps and team scores for tournaments. He tried explaining the math behind golfing handicaps, which were designed to make it possible for less-experienced golfers to be competitive with better golfers. But as soon he got to the breakdown per hole and calculating team handicaps, Julie shook her head and walked away with a wave, humming loudly as if to block him out. Fair enough. It wasn't as if she'd need to know any of that right away.

He gave her a tour of the small kitchen, which was basically set up for burgers, hot dogs, chicken wraps and cold sandwiches. If they had a tournament going on, they had warming ovens for prepared foods the resort kitchen would supply—baked ziti, chicken casserole, roast turkey, even prime rib on occasion. Their final stop was the storeroom, which was overflowing with catering supplies like tablecloths and dishes as well as shop inventory, scorecards, and pretty much anything small the course might need.

The cluttered room he'd been using for weeks to distract himself from his attraction to Julie had a whole different vibe when she was standing in the middle of it. He'd have to come up with something else from now on. Maybe thoughts of the dentist. He shuddered. That would do it.

As if reading his mind, Julie walked past him and patted his arm.

"Let's get back to the pro shop, where we can't be tempted to, um, be spontaneous again."

He agreed, but he couldn't shake his feeling of regret as he locked the door behind them. He could not start imagining kissing Julie against that stack of chairs. Or against the door.

No kissing thoughts at all.

Julie knew the weekend was going to be a challenge as soon as she saw Blake leaving the resort in a hurry that Friday afternoon, his face a distressing shade of green. Blake Randall *never* got sick. Then Amanda sent a text, declaring their home next to the resort a *quarantine center* to be avoided at all costs. Their teenage son, Zach, had apparently brought the stomach flu home from the summer camp where he worked and all four of them were now sick, including seven-year-old Maddy.

Okay. Julie went into the break room and stared

at the schedule wall. *I can do this*. It wasn't like Blake and Amanda were that hands-on as managers, but on the weekends they pitched in wherever needed. Julie couldn't shake the feeling that this was the beginning of an avalanche.

Sure enough, the phone began to ring as the afternoon went on. Kitchen staff. Housekeeping. Front-desk workers. The good news was the only wedding that weekend was scheduled for Sunday afternoon, so maybe some workers would be back by then. But they had that corporate golf tournament on Saturday, so the resort would be busy all weekend.

She called the temp agency in White Plains that she sometimes used around the holidays and arranged for enough temps to at least keep the rooms clean and food served. Nick West would be busy covering for two of his security staff who were sick, but Cassie offered to help at the front desk. Julie and Katie could work with Housekeeping and the temps. She'd have to work some long hours, but that was hardly unusual on a weekend. She'd take an extra day off once things got back to normal.

There were a few hiccups getting people checked in, but nothing major. It was nothing the guests seemed to notice or care about. Everyone was in good spirits and when Julie finally headed home that night, she was feeling pretty confident. She'd heard Jerry at the golf course was sick, but Quinn could probably handle the tournament on his own. He'd have to hustle, but…welcome to the club.

Her phone rang just before six the next morning. The screen showed Katie Walker's name, and she groaned. There was only one reason why she'd be calling this early—she was sick, too.

"Katie? It's okay if you're sick. We'll manage…" She wasn't sure how, but she'd juggle the schedule somehow.

"It's not just me, Julie." Katie's voice cracked. "I started it, but now Dad's sick, too. This place turned into a hell house overnight."

"*Quinn* is sick?" Her mind stuttered to a halt. "What about the tournament?" That didn't sound very nice. "I mean…is he okay?"

"That's why I'm calling." Katie moaned. "Oh, hang on… I'm gonna be…" There was silence, and Julie thought they'd been disconnected, but Katie came back. "False alarm. But I can hear Dad upstairs right now and it is *not* pretty. There is no way he'll be there. He tossed a note downstairs to me." She moaned again, then took a shaky breath. Julie wondered if she should go over there to help, but if *she* got sick, they might as well shut down the resort at this point. Katie coughed, then her voice steadied. "Dad said it's like running a wedding, and you do that all the time. Said it's all about logistics. All the scorecards and sign-up sheets are in a folder on the counter. Ugh…hang on, I dropped his note… Got it. Oh, yeah—you have to be there to open the pro shop by seven. And he says he's really sorry, but—and I quote—'you got this.'" Before Julie could say anything, Katie muttered, "Uh-oh…gotta go…" and the line went dead.

After taking a moment to collect her thoughts, Julie jumped out of bed, earning herself a dirty look from Fluff. She'd set out a suit to wear, but grabbed a cute floral golf set instead. She might as well look the part if she was going to run a golf tournament. *Oh, God.* She was running a golf tournament. She texted Cassie with the news that Cassie would be in charge at the resort, then drove to the golf club. She should have paid more attention to that whole handicap equation Quinn had talked about, since it was pretty important to the game of golf. Maybe someone from the tournament could help her with that.

She had the shop open before the first players arrived, and she did her best to sound somewhat knowledgeable as she signed them up and handed them their cards and the preprinted schedules for the tournament. That was the easy part. Things wouldn't get interesting until *after* everyone played and she had to calculate which team actually won. She was busy checking out a few purchases golfers were making when she heard a familiar voice behind her.

"I heard you might need a hand." Shane Brannigan took the folder from the counter. "Is this the tourney folder? Yup." He answered his own question, turning to help a foursome of golfers who'd just walked in. Shane was a sports agent *and* a good golfer. Julie knew him as Mel's husband, but he was also Quinn's friend. And thankfully, the tall, handsome redhead looked very healthy.

Once the tournament players had gotten off to start their games, Julie handed Shane a coffee and leaned against the counter with a heavy sigh. "You're a lifesaver. Can you handle things here for a bit while I go check on how Cassie's doing at the resort?"

"I'm here all day, so do what you need to do." Shane patted her on the shoulder.

"Did Katie tell you I was going to be in way over my head today?"

"Quinn texted me and said you'd need someone to handle the scoring." Shane took a sip of his coffee and chuckled. "He also said he'd been lying on the bathroom floor since three o'clock this morning."

"Ugh. I wish I could go over and help him and Katie, but—"

"Don't even think about it. Mel said the same thing about going to help Blake and Amanda, but those of us who are still standing need to stay that way. They'll all be fine. It's a fast bug." He checked the clock. "Go do what you need to do. I'll hold down the fort here."

Julie spent the rest of the day dashing back and

forth between the resort and the clubhouse, making sure everything got done on schedule and that guests would never know how short-staffed they were. She was exhausted by midafternoon. The temporary employees were doing a good job, with only the occasional bobble. She made a note to herself to be sure to send flowers to the agency for saving the weekend. Thankfully, the resort chef, Dario, was fit as a fiddle, and he had most of his kitchen staff on hand. So the restaurant and banquet room were open and running relatively smoothly.

Still, she didn't dare let down her guard. She made regular circuits around all the facilities and departments to keep workers' spirits up, fill in if someone needed a break and answer any questions. Couldn't find the vodka? She directed the temp bartender to the proper storage room. No queen sheets on the second-floor east wing? Julie grabbed them from the laundry and rushed them up to the housekeeper. Vacuum cleaner stopped working on the third-floor west wing? She pulled a new one from the basement storage room and carried it up, bringing the broken one back down to the basement again. All the running was making her sweat.

She was back at the golf club as the golfers finished to help Shane collect scorecards and to make sure the luncheon was hot and ready, and that the bar was well-stocked and fully staffed. She and Shane handed out the trophies, posing for photographs with the winning teams. There were smiles all around. They'd done it.

She kept guzzling water to stay cool. She made a note to ask Quinn if the air-conditioning worked properly in the clubhouse. He'd been texting both her and Shane all day with reminders, tips and questions, and they'd both started ignoring him. The man needed to rest and stop stressing himself *and* them. It wasn't until the evening was winding down that Julie allowed herself a moment to sit on the veranda overlooking the dark lake and close her eyes. She had no idea where her tablet and folder of receipts were, but she'd worry about that tomorrow. She'd grabbed little snacks here and there all day but hadn't taken the time for an actual meal. That was probably just as well, as she was beginning to feel a little queasy. Not *sick*, but *off*. She figured it was exhaustion catching up to her, since she hadn't had a day *this* busy in ages.

She pulled out her phone and texted more thank-yous to Cassie, Nick, Shane and staffers who'd gone above and beyond. Amanda texted back that the Randall household was beginning to recover. Blake had bounced back the fastest and would be at the resort in the morning, but little Maddy was still miserable. And, of course, she had a long string of unanswered texts from Quinn.

Did you find the prize certificates in the office?

Don't forget we're supposed to serve lunch after they golf.

Is everything going okay?

Hello?

Come on—tell me what's happening.

Julie rolled her eyes at the screen, then regretted it immediately. Things were already tilting around her, and rolling her eyes made her feel seasick. She felt dehydrated, but she'd had so much water. She decided she'd better reassure Quinn and started typing.

No offense, but we survived just fine without you. Golfers and guests are happy. Now stop testing mu. Go slepe.

She was frowning at her typos when he responded.

Testing mu? Are you okay?

Of course, he'd pick up on her mistake.

I'm peshy. Just tire

She'd hit Send before seeing more typos. She meant to say she was *peachy*. But the screen was swirling almost as much as the veranda was. *Weird*. She couldn't deny the truth any longer. She was more than just exhausted. She was sick. Coming out here to sit alone wasn't a great idea. Her phone chirped.

Peshy? Are you home?

Home would be nice right about now. She didn't know how she'd drive, but first she needed to get to the parking lot. The golf-club parking lot, which was a long walk in the dark, but that was where she'd parked her car this morning. Maybe the fresh air would help wake her up. She stood, willing her more-than-just-queasy stomach to behave itself until she could get home. Her phone chirped again as she headed across the resort lawn.

Where are you?????

Oh, yeah. Quinn. She hadn't answered his question the first time. She leaned against a tree, still using sheer willpower to keep from being sick. Quinn would tell her she was being a control freak again, but it was working so far, even if it took every bit of strength she had. She tapped her answer, taking the time to proofread it so he wouldn't think she was drunk. Just the thought of alcohol made her stomach heave, but she gritted her teeth and held on as she sent the text.

Heading to car now. Go to bed, worrywart. I'm fine.

Her ability to control the doom she knew was coming ran out just as she got her car in sight. It was the only one left in the clubhouse lot. Her phone kept chirping with texts, but she ignored them. The club itself was locked up tight, but there were plenty of lights around the lot. All she had to do was get to her little blue sedan and drive home. She had this.

Except she didn't. Why didn't anyone mention this flu bug made them so damned dizzy and fuzzy-headed and…*oh, no*…sick? She threw up at the edge of the lot, clutching the base of a light pole.

Thank God no one was around to see this humiliation. She got sick again, and tears spilled onto her cheeks. The violence of the nausea made her hurt all over. This was going to be a long, miserable night. What if no one found her until morning?

This wouldn't work at all. She had to get to her car. She had to keep it together for just ten more minutes so she could get home to warmth and safety. She pulled herself up straight. *I will not be sick. I will not be sick.* Why were there lights moving in front of her? Was she hallucinating? All she had to do was walk to her car. One step at a time.

It only took one step to set off another tidal wave in her stomach. She dropped to one knee, sick again. Crying again. And scared. There was movement, or was she just dizzy? She heard her name and felt arms around her. She sagged into the embrace, trying to mumble a warning before getting ill again. A familiar voice came from above her, sounding amused, but also blessedly calm and in control. "It's okay. I've got you."

Chapter Ten

Quinn hadn't felt this sleep-deprived since those long weeks after losing Anne. His body ached with exhaustion after being awake for twenty-six hours straight, but at least he was able to relax a little now that Julie seemed to be in a peaceful sleep at last. He hadn't dared let himself sleep until he knew Julie was past the worst of it.

He'd left the course on Friday afternoon to pick up Katie from her friend's house. He had to stop the car twice on the way home for her to get sick, and he'd taken care of her at home as she cried and retched for hours. He hated feeling so helpless— even when it was just a stomach flu, no parent wants to see their child like that. Katie went to sleep just before midnight. An hour later, he woke up to his own loudly grumbling stomach and a spinning room. He kept telling himself it could not happen, but that didn't work for long. He was kneeling on the bathroom floor by three in the morning.

He felt awful for putting all the work of the golf tournament on Julie and Shane, but he figured with her organizing skills and Shane's golf experience, they'd figure it out. And from what he'd heard from some of the golfers there, everything had gone smoothly on their end. He didn't like hearing that Julie had insisted on running both the resort and the club, but that was Julie—she needed to be the Woman In Charge.

There was a soft whimper from the bed in front of him, and Julie rolled over, pulling a colorful pastel quilt up over her shoulders. Quinn reached for the nearby bucket lined with a plastic bag, but her eyes never opened—she just sighed and went back to sleep. The worst of the bug seemed to be behind her. He shifted in the kitchen chair he'd carried into her room so he could keep an eye on her.

He wasn't sure what made him realize she was coming down with the flu last night. A few typos normally wouldn't be a big deal in a text, but Julie rarely misspelled anything. She didn't even use the usual texting abbreviations like *CU* for *see you* or

TKS for *thanks*. Proper communication at all times. That was his Julie.

Quinn straightened. Not *his* Julie.

But what else made him jump in his car and go looking for her? He knew something was off with her. Maybe it was just exhaustion from a crazy-busy day, which was partly his fault. Or maybe she was having the same sweat-then-chills dizzy spells that he'd had in the middle of the night, which meant she shouldn't be driving. When he'd spotted her on her knees by the parking lot light, his heart had just about jumped out of his chest. She was alone. And sick. She'd barely mumbled a greeting before getting sick down the front of his shirt. He'd carried her to his car. Somehow they made it back to her place before she got sick again, but just barely.

He'd helped Julie out of her soiled clothes as soon as they got to her house. Normally that would be a sentence fraught with innuendo, but only a complete jerk would be thinking that way when she was barely able to stand. And he didn't touch her underwear.

He'd slipped a nightshirt over her head, doing his best not to look anywhere he shouldn't. He treated her the same as he'd treated Katie when she was sick—set her up with some cushions on the bathroom floor near the toilet and had a stack of cool, damp washcloths handy. He tossed her clothes and his shirt in the wash. Then he'd sat on the floor in the corner, where he could keep an eye on her. He held her hair back when needed, put a cool cloth to her forehead, tried to get her to sip some water and covered her up when she lay down again. Julie was going to be in that bathroom most of the night. Which meant he would be, too.

He'd texted Katie to let her know he wouldn't be back home. He'd texted Blake to let him know Julie wouldn't be able to work at the resort on Sunday. To his surprise, Blake didn't ask any questions about why *Quinn* was telling him this. He'd simply replied that he and Amanda were both feeling better and could handle things.

He'd helped Julie to bed just after dawn. She was mumbling apologies until she fell asleep. He'd kept the bucket nearby, just in case, but she'd barely moved. And he'd watched over her every breath, determined not to sleep until he knew she was okay. A few of her friends had offered to take his place, but he'd told them there was no need for them to be exposed. He'd already been sick. It was more logical for him to stay.

He sat on the edge of Julie's bed and felt her forehead—no fever. There was no reason he couldn't catch a nap for a few hours, but...where? Julie's living room sofa was too short for him to stretch out on comfortably. She had a guest bedroom, but there were boxes and papers stacked on the bed in there. He'd taken a closer look—couldn't help being curious—and discovered it was a class project of some sort. Blake said she was going for her MBA, and this seemed to be data from a study she was doing on creating an online consulting business. No way was he going to touch that to clear space to sleep.

Quinn turned from where he was sitting on her bed and leaned against a pillow he'd propped on the headboard. It was a king-size bed. There was plenty of room for him to stretch his legs and close his eyes for just a few minutes as he sat there. A quick catnap, that was all. Julie sighed in her sleep and turned toward him, her dark hair falling over her face. He reached over and brushed it back, but she didn't even flinch. She was so out of it that she'd never know he was there, and there was at least a foot of space separating them. She was under the covers, and he was sitting on top of them. He just needed to close his eyes for a little while...

The first thing Julie noticed when she blinked awake was that it was daytime. She could hear it raining outside. She felt as limp as a dishrag. And her mouth felt dry and...nasty. She ran her tongue along her lips, which felt chapped. She blinked a few more times and tried to put the pieces together.

She'd been at the resort, working in overdrive into the night because everyone was sick. Then *she'd* started to feel sick. She remembered heading for the parking lot at the golf club, but things got fuzzy after that. It was like watching a streamed movie on a laptop with bad WiFi—the images kept freezing or digitizing into a blur, and the sound kept cutting in and out. She had been sick by the lamppost and remembered being grateful no one was around. But…someone *was* there. Someone called her name, and she'd felt strong arms around her. Was that *Quinn*? She closed her eyes tightly. How embarrassing!

Somehow she'd gotten home, but she didn't remember driving. Thank God she hadn't had an accident. She remembered being on the bathroom floor, but she didn't recall bringing in the pillows she'd been lying on. She'd been sick. A lot. That was a downside to living alone. No one to comfort you in times like that. Except…it seemed someone *had* been there. She remembered someone putting cool compresses on her forehead. Low words of comfort. A glass of water pressed to her lips.

Julie stretched, feeling a bit of life flowing back to her limbs. She was aching and exhausted. It must be the fever that made her imagine it had been a man's voice telling her she'd be okay. That it had sounded like Quinn Walker's voice, which was impossible. For one thing, he'd been sick himself. And for another, well…it just didn't make any sense. She forced herself upright to sit on the edge of the bed, blinking as the room went hazy, then snapped into focus again. There was a glass of water on her nightstand and she grabbed for it. She wanted to guzzle the whole thing, but she knew that was a bad idea on an empty, traumatized stomach, so she carefully sipped it.

She didn't see her phone anywhere, which was odd. She normally charged it on her nightstand and used it as her alarm. They'd probably already figured out at the resort that she was *not* showing up, but she still needed to call Blake to apologize and see if things were under control. Funny…she didn't see her clothes from yesterday, either. She was in an old nightshirt she hardly ever wore in warmer weather, but she must have managed to change into it somehow.

The soft shushing sound of sheets moving behind her sent a bolt of alarm up her spine, before she realized what it must be.

"G'morning, Fluff. Nice to know you cared enough to stay."

Instead of hearing a purr, she heard a man's grumbled moan.

She jumped up off the bed with a strangled cry and spun, looking around wildly for anything she could use as a weapon.

It was *Quinn*. Shirtless. In. Her. Bed.

Her sudden movement hadn't woken him. He was on his side, facing her, with his face looking nearly angelic in repose…except for the fact that he'd taken off his shirt and crawled into her bed! Technically he was *on* the bed, not under the covers. And, while his shirt was missing, he did have his jeans and socks on. A thick wave of hair fell across his forehead. His eyelashes were thick and dark against his cheek. The shadow of his unshaven jawline made the chiseled lines of his face more handsome than ever. And his chest was nearly as chiseled as that jawline, with a soft covering of dark hair that she was dying to run her fingers through.

She stepped farther away from the bed. *No touching!*

What the ever-loving hell was he doing here?

And then the missing pieces of her memory fell into place with a resounding click. It *had* been him in the parking lot. He'd carried her to his car and into her house. He'd changed her clothes. Oh, God. He'd *changed her clothes*. Her cheeks went red-hot. She didn't remember every detail of the long night, but she knew without a doubt that it was Quinn who'd held her when she was sick. Quinn who'd cooled her face with a damp cloth. Quinn who'd quietly urged her to drink water to hydrate. And it was Quinn who'd tucked her into bed. The dress incident was embarrassing enough—how would she ever survive *this* level of humiliation?

He grumbled something in his sleep and rolled onto his back, covering his face with one arm. The pose made his chest and shoulder muscles bunch together, and his jeans sagged lower on his waist. He looked like a model in a very sexy ad campaign. Whatever he was selling, Julie wanted it. But right now he didn't even know she was there, staring at him with lust on her mind. She stepped back again. It was creepy for her to be inventorying his body when he was basically unconscious. But…*damn*. He looked good in her bed.

Practicality set in eventually. She had to find her phone and call the resort. She had to take a shower, brush her teeth a few dozen times and get dressed. And then she'd wake Quinn. As she showered, letting the hot steam envelop her, she thought about how exhausted he must have been. He and Katie had been sick all Friday night and into Saturday, then he'd come to rescue her and stayed with her all night. She peeked into the room to make sure he was still asleep before dashing into her walk-in closet with her towel wrapped around her.

She was surprised to find Quinn sitting up and rubbing his eyes when she stepped back into the bedroom. When he saw her, he started to smile, then seemed to realize where he was. You know… in her *bed*. He stood, looking stricken.

"Oh, damn. What time is it? What…?" His gaze ran down her body. "You're dressed. And showered. You feel okay?" She nodded, but before she could answer, he stared down at the bed as if it had behaved very badly and he was disappointed in it.

"I was just going to close my eyes for a second, I swear. And I stayed on this side, away from you." His eyes went wide. "Didn't I?"

Mr. Spontaneous was in a panic. "You did. Take a breath before you hyperventilate. It's a little after twelve, and yes, I've taken a shower and am feeling a *lot* better. Other than the humiliation, of course, which I'll probably never recover from."

His eyes were kind, and the caring expression made her chest go warm. "There's nothing to be humiliated about. You can't help it if you caught the same bug that half the town came down with."

He had a point, and she felt some of her tension ease. Maybe this wasn't as disastrous as she'd thought. She walked around the bed toward both him and the doorway. She stopped at his side, giving him an exaggerated once-over with her eyes.

"I can't help wondering where your shirt went."

He shrugged, playfulness gleaming in his eyes. "Right now it's in your clothes dryer, along with your clothes from last night. I washed them when we got here, because, well…"

Julie felt herself dying a little inside as more missing pieces of the night came to her. She'd been *so* sick when he found her. She'd thanked him by vomiting all over his shirt. Nope—she was definitely not going to survive this. She covered her face with her hands and groaned loudly.

"Oh, my God, I remember. I got…well, I, um,

all over you." Her voice faded to a near whisper. "Excuse me while I go crawl under a rock and stay there for the rest of my life."

"Not going to happen." He gently tugged her hands away from her face, smiling as he held on to them. "It's an absolute set-in-stone rule that no one is responsible for what they do or say when they're in the throes of a feverish stomach flu. You get a full pass *and* a vow of silence. It's no one else's business what happened, and they'll never hear about it from me." His fingers lifted her chin so that she was staring right into his eyes. "You were *sick*. Stop beating yourself up. Got it?"

They stared at each other, the room silent other than the sound of the frantic racing of her heart. Was he going to kiss her again? She wanted him to. She wanted him to kiss away her shame, her doubts and her conviction that they would be wrong for each other.

Quinn stepped closer. His Adam's apple bobbed up and down as he swallowed hard. He was just beginning to lower his head toward hers. *Yes, please.* Her fingertips were just grazing his chest when her phone started ringing somewhere. She wanted to ignore it and concentrate on that expanse of hard muscle. But it was her brother's ringtone. If she didn't answer, Bobby would show up at her door, which would lead to a whole lot of questions she wouldn't know how to answer. She stepped back, her voice—and heart—full of regret.

"That's my brother." She looked around the room. "Do you know where my phone is?"

"I set it on the kitchen table before tossing our clothes in the laundry."

She brushed by him with a whispered apology. She was sure she heard him mumble a curse as she hurried to the kitchen. *Same, Quinn. Same.*

"Hi, Bobby."

"Sis! I heard you caught that bug." He had her on the speakerphone in his truck. "You okay? You need anything? I'm heading up to the ski lodge to finish a job for Matt, but I can stop by—"

"No, don't come over!" Julie almost shouted her answer. She heard a snort of laughter behind her from Quinn. Her voice lowered. "I mean… I'm fine. Don't interrupt your day for me. It wasn't a great night, but I'm good now, I promise." Another snort from Quinn. She flipped her middle finger in the air and he barked out a short laugh, which her brother heard.

"Is someone there with you?"

She made a face at Quinn and waved her hand to shush him. He'd grabbed his shirt from the laundry, covering that enticing chest of his. "I've got an old movie on the television," Julie told her brother. "Just doing a pamper day—hot tea, a good book, a

Hollywood musical and as many naps as I can work in. Who told you I was sick?"

He laughed. "You know how it works in this town. Matt heard it from Jillie, Jillie heard it from Mackenzie, Mack heard it from Nora and Nora heard it from Amanda. Hey, I'm just pulling into the lodge. How about I have Matt's cook make one of those turkey sandwiches you like so much when I'm done, and I'll drop it off?"

Julie gave Quinn a sad look. If it wasn't Bobby stopping by, it would be one of her friends. Any thoughts of grabbing a little escape with Quinn this afternoon evaporated, and he knew it from her expression. "Sure. That'd be great, Bob. Don't hurry, though."

She put the phone down with a heavy sigh. "If it's not him, it would be—"

"Any one of your friends checking on you. I get it. It's a Sunday afternoon and people are worried. You're lucky to have so many people who care about you."

"I guess you're right." But today she only wanted one person to care for her.

"Let me make you some scrambled eggs before I go. Do you want coffee?"

"No, Quinn. I'll make myself some toast, and Bobby's bringing food later." She straightened her shoulders and regathered her common sense. The sooner Quinn left, the sooner she'd be able to get some more sleep and snap out of this uncharacteristically reckless mood she was in. "I think it's best if you go, so we don't have to make awkward explanations to anyone. Or make any stupid mistakes."

He stepped closer. "You're probably right, but Julie, I meant what I said about exploring whatever this is between us. I mean, not a forever thing, but maybe…once. Just for each of us to get…back in the swing of things, so to speak."

"I must be a little feverish." Julie put her hand on his chest so he couldn't come closer. "Because it sounds like you're suggesting that you and I…do more than kiss?"

He shrugged. "I'm just sayin' maybe that would stop our…curiosity. Then we'd know if we were… ready for the market."

Her laughter bubbled up. "That is the most unromantic offer I've ever heard."

He put his hand over hers. "That's the whole point—no romance. We know each other, we trust each other and we might even *like* each other a little, so…"

"I don't think so, Quinn." She gave his chest a gentle push and pulled her hand back. "We've agreed before that you and I are a mistake, and that didn't change just because we had a moment of horniness and thought about having an afternoon tumble."

His eyebrow rose. "Afternoon tumble? I think

I could provide something more memorable than that."

She didn't doubt it. But...*bad idea.*

"Quinn, we're both exhausted and in a weird place after being sick. I know you like being spontaneous, but neither of us should be making potentially disastrous decisions right now. We need to be clearheaded and sure of ourselves." He smiled now, and there was a strong hint of mischief to it. "What?"

"You haven't ruled us out."

"There is no *us*, Quinn." She wasn't even convincing herself.

He swept in to cup her face with his hands and kissed her hard, making her tingle right down to her toes. His smile was even deeper when he released her and opened her front door.

"But there could be."

you and Julie. She runs my resort. You run
olf course. The two of you having a relation-
opens up all kinds of scary…" He gave Quinn
ck, rueful glance. "And *wonderful* workplace
arios. Look, Amanda was my interior designer
n we fell in love, so sort of my employee. Nick
Cassie fell in love while working at the re-
It happens. I'm not saying *don't*, but, dude…
areful."

We're not having a relationship. I found out she
sick and I made sure she got home okay. Yes,
yed the night, but you know what the first few
s of that bug was like…" Blake shuddered with
unt. Quinn continued. "The exact opposite of
antic, right? After I texted you this morning,
finally fell asleep. I was so tired that I dozed
too. That's it."

hat wasn't exactly *it*, but it was as much as he
willing to share. Blake wasn't buying it, though.
You just happened to spend the whole night tak-
care of the woman, fell asleep in her house,
you expect me to believe that's it? This is Julie
e talking about—the one you've argued with
hree years. And you're the guy who said you
n't ready for dating, but now you're rushing to
escue?"

We're not dating. Not even *talking* about dat-
" He jammed his fingers through his hair. "It
just a kiss. That's all."

Chapter Eleven

"Dad!" Katie's voice came from the house. "We
have company!"

Thinking it might be Julie, Quinn scrambled to
his feet from his seat at the end of the dock. He'd
been sitting out there for an hour or so, watching
the late-June sun slowly settle toward the mountains across the lake. The rain had passed by midafternoon. He'd hoped the fresh air and the calming
sound of the waves lapping at the shore behind him
would help him figure out what to do now that he'd
dropped that wild suggestion on Julie.

But it wasn't Julie who strode out of the house
and down to the dock. It was his boss.

"Feeling better?" Blake asked. "Amanda thought you two might appreciate some dinner you didn't have to cook yourselves." He sat down on the bench and Quinn joined him. "She made about a dozen shepherd's pie casseroles today, and we're delivering them all over town."

"Wow, thanks. I hadn't even thought about dinner yet." That might be partly due to the aftereffects of the stomach bug, but he suspected it was more because he couldn't stop thinking about Julie Brown. "Is Amanda inside with Katie?"

"No, we decided to divide and conquer. I think she's at Julie's now. I told Katie how to warm up the food." Blake was looking out over the lake, but he gave Quinn a sideways glance. "Speaking of Julie…"

He knew Blake was going to have questions about his text. But he hadn't anticipated a house visit that very same day. He tried deflection first.

"How did things go at the resort today? Were there any issues at the golf club? Any more staff fall ill?"

Blake looked amused, but he went along. "We had a few more people call in sick, but some of the first ones were able to come in today, so it worked out. I don't think there were any issues that guests would have picked up on."

"I'm glad. Uh…how are *you* feeling? Are the kids okay?"

"Friday night was *not* a hap[…] maced. "Zach started it. Then [...] with it, poor little peanut. Am[...] after midnight, and I got it a few [...] know, that bug was no fun."

Quinn looked out at the water [...] beginning to graze the top of the [...] started it here. I thought maybe [...] avoid it. No such luck."

Blake nodded and pursed his li[...] managed to get to Julie's place las[...]

Quinn straightened. Was this ab[...] but not until late. I really couldn[...] the day… You know I'd never sla[...] erwise—"

"Relax," Blake said. "Of course, [...] stared down at the dock for a mon[...] toward Quinn. "Your personal li[...] business, but the resort does hav[...] fraternization, so I have to ask if [...] you know."

"Fraternization? Trust me, ther[...] of that happening." Although the [...] close this morning. "And she ar[...] supervisor-and-subordinate positi[...]

"Argh…" Blake scrubbed his [...] face. "I hate these conversations.[...] sigh. "This isn't an official discu[...] I would like a heads-up if someth[...]

"Whoa…you *kissed* her? When did this happen?"

Quinn swore under his breath. He did *not* mean to mention the kiss out loud. He gave Blake a hard look. "Remember that bit about my private life not being any of your business?"

"Dad!" Katie called out from the house, breaking the stare-down between the two men. "Dinner in five minutes!"

He waved in answer and started to stand, but Blake stopped him.

"Forget about our respective jobs and the resort and all the stuff that doesn't matter. Man to man—how do you feel about Julie?"

Quinn blinked. That was a good question. "There's something between us, but I can't put words to it. I'm not sure if it's real or if it's just me getting lonely for the company of a woman."

"You've been alone a long time. But I swear to God—" Blake's voice hardened "—if you're just looking to scratch an itch, do it with someone else. Julie deserves better."

"Look, I *care* about Julie. I don't want to hurt her. She and I would go into it with clear eyes."

Blake's eyebrows rose. "So you two have already talked about doing…something?"

Quinn didn't answer. That was between him and Julie.

"O-kay." Blake patted Quinn's back as they headed off the dock. "You keep saying there's something between you. If there's a chance that could be something serious…well, all I can say is don't blow it."

After all the drama of the weekend, the only thing Julie wanted was a nice quiet Monday of solitude. But the universe apparently didn't receive her memo. The first to arrive at her door was Amanda, which wasn't unusual for a Monday morning, so Julie couldn't really complain. She'd made some beer bread the night before, so they had slices of that slathered with butter and honey, just the way Nanny used to make it after Julie or Bobby had been sick as kids.

Amanda was still bursting with questions about Quinn, same as when she'd stopped by with a small casserole yesterday. But Julie wasn't ready to say much, other than that he'd taken care of her all night, he'd been a perfect gentleman and then he'd left. She didn't mention that he'd floated a wild suggestion that they sleep together…just to see what might happen. Julie needed to figure out how she felt about that idea herself before gathering more opinions on it, even from her best friend.

There was always the chance it had been his lack of rest and flu recovery that prompted the idea that they "practice" their skills. He might never bring it up again, and that would probably be for the best. She blinked. Not *probably*—*definitely* for the best.

It would affect their work relationship, their newly founded friendship, their relationships with their friends… Sleeping with Quinn had *disaster* written all over it. Which was why it made no sense that she couldn't stop thinking about it.

She maintained her most interested expression as Amanda talked about her upcoming getaway weekend with Blake. How people didn't understand that owners of a resort needed vacations, too. They were headed to Quebec for a few days of being simply tourists.

Amanda somehow managed to intersperse mentions of Quinn in every other sentence as she rattled on. Quinn was busy, too. Quinn and Blake were planning a new tournament that fall. Quinn had suggested Quebec because he'd taken Katie there last year. Quinn was teaching Zach how to golf. Finally Julie leveled a look at her friend.

"You're as subtle as a sledgehammer, Amanda. Stop."

"I have no idea what you mean." Amanda played innocent, going so far as to dramatically put her hand on her chest to show her shock.

"There's nothing more to tell you about Quinn and me. Yes, we've become friends, I guess." She set her coffee mug on the table. "But he's made it clear he's not ready to start a relationship with anyone, and I'm looking for more than an afternoon shag."

Amanda laughed. "An *afternoon shag*? That's

a little specific. There's no shame in having some fun. You're not a virgin, Julie. You don't need to save yourself for The One."

"Thanks for the permission, Mom." Julie stood and took their dishes to the sink. "But that's never been my style. If I don't see a future with a guy, why would I let him in my bedroom?"

"Well, Quinn's already *been* in your bedroom, right?"

She turned and put her hand on her hip. "Yeah. He was in my bedroom watching me retch for hours. Not exactly a sexy scenario. Give it up, Amanda."

After she left, Julie finally had the house to herself. She settled into her recliner with a book. Less than fifteen minutes later, her brother knocked on the door, wearing his tool belt.

Bobby gave her a big smile. "The screen door for your back entrance came in, so I figured today would be a good day to install it."

Power tools were *not* the ambiance she was going for on this pamper-herself day, but she loved her brother and she was lucky that he did so many projects for her, large and small. She ushered him to the back door, and an hour later, made him lunch. They sat on her small deck to eat.

"The yard looks good, sis. Very organized."

"What does *that* mean?"

Bobby brushed his long blond hair off his forehead, looking confused. "The *yard* is that expanse of greenery." He gestured, speaking in a voice a child would use with a silly adult. "*Good* means nice or attractive. And *organized* means the plants are symmetrical and complement each other, just the way you planned." He winked playfully. "Are there any other definitions I can help you with?"

She threw her napkin at him. "Smart-ass. It's just that I know I can be a little obsessive about my organization."

He thought about that, his smile fading. "That's just how you keep things in your life manageable."

"I've been told I need to be more spontaneous."

"Told by who?"

By the man who wants to sleep with me for fun.

"Doesn't matter," she answered. "It just made me wonder, that's all."

Bobby took a swig of the beer she'd brought out for him. "You like order in your life. That's why you're such a great manager. I build things, which also requires some sense of order and logic. We're products of our past."

They rarely talked about their childhood, with the exception of memories of Nanny. Even then, they tended to skirt around the reason she'd come into their lives in the first place. They remembered her cooking because they wouldn't have eaten a cooked meal without her. They remembered her hugs because she was the only one who'd given them.

Julie started gathering their plates. "And look at

us…thirty-nine and forty-three and never married. Maybe that *control* thing isn't working as well as we thought."

Bobby looked surprised. "It was never meant to be a relationship-builder. It was meant to protect us. Those two things don't always go all that well together." He leaned forward. "What's going on? Is everything okay?"

"Everything's fine." She waved him off. "I'm just worn-out from being sick yesterday, and I'm feeling sorry for myself."

"Sis, when the time is right, you and I will find our people. We're just late bloomers, that's all. But I'm hopin' it'll be worth the wait."

Julie stood and nodded toward the screen door leaning against the house. "I hope so, too. Meanwhile, I'm in serious need of a nap and that can't happen while you're working."

It was another hour before Bobby finished and headed back to his place. He told her when he left that he needed a different type of lock for the door, and he had one at home. He'd stop by during the week to finish it up. Julie took a quick nap, then warmed up the leftover shepherd's pie for dinner.

Just because the day hadn't been as quiet as she'd hoped, that didn't mean she couldn't still be self-indulgent. She filled the bathtub and soaked in rose-scented bubbles for a while, then rubbed moisturizing cream over her body after she dried off.

Her hair could air-dry, even if it meant it would dry wavy. No one would see her. It was almost seven when she tugged on her favorite pajamas and an old chenille robe. The ten-year-old robe was long and warm and felt like a security blanket.

After pouring herself a glass of wine to go along with her bowl of chips, she curled up once again in her recliner and picked up the book. She'd eat healthy tomorrow.

The knock at the door, soft as it was, almost made her spill her wine. It was eight o'clock. She looked down at the worn robe and the ancient Birkenstocks she was wearing as slippers. *Very attractive.* She shrugged to herself. It didn't matter how she looked, since it had to be Bobby with the new lock.

She was picking a piece of potato chip from her robe as she opened the door, but it dropped from her fingers when she saw Quinn Walker standing on the steps.

They stared at each other in stunned silence until the corners of Quinn's mouth quirked upward.

"You definitely have a unique way of greeting people at the door." He paused. "I have something for you."

Chapter Twelve

It had never been Quinn's style to show up and stake a claim. Anne used to laugh that *she* had to be the one to ask for *his* number when they met. Maybe it was because he was out of practice. Maybe it was because Julie made him stop caring about who he *used* to be and made him think only of what he wanted right here and right now.

He held out her tablet and a manila folder. "You left this on my desk. I thought you might need it."

He'd spent the day distracted with thoughts of her. Thoughts of the crazy suggestion that had come out of his mouth. *Let's do it and see what happens.* There was a big difference between spontaneous and reckless, and he'd veered very far toward the latter. But she hadn't shut him down. Oh, she'd stopped him in the moment, and presented a reasonable argument why they shouldn't. Friendship. Work. Blah, blah, blah. But she hadn't said never. She'd just said they should think about it. Should be sure.

One thing Quinn was sure of by the end of the day was that he wasn't going to rest until he knew where her head was at. She was a woman who liked order and control, so he fully expected her to shut him down. If she truly wasn't interested, that was that. Except...he couldn't help feeling like Julie *was* interested.

When he'd seen her tablet sitting in his office, along with a folder of receipts from the resort, he figured it was a good excuse to see her. It could certainly wait until she got back to work on Tuesday, but there might be something urgent in that tablet. She might be worried about where it was. She might still be thinking about his proposition. Which was why he'd jumped into his car and headed to her house after dinner. He just wanted to know one way or the other, for his own sanity.

She'd opened the door in that bathrobe with her dark hair pinned on top of her head with a clip, wavy strands falling around her face, and his simple question slipped right out of his mind.

She took the tablet and stared at it as if she didn't

recognize it. "You thought I'd need my tablet on a Monday night?"

"Well, uh…" he stuttered. "I didn't want you getting to work tomorrow not knowing where it was."

Her eyes narrowed. "You could have put it on my desk. And I'm off tomorrow—Blake gave me a personal day after everything that happened over the weekend."

"I thought maybe you'd worry about where it was." She was making him work for this.

She gave him a sarcastic grin. "How thoughtful. Thanks."

And there they stood. She still hadn't moved. Hadn't invited him in. She hadn't slapped his face and shoved him down the steps, either. She just stared into his eyes as if she was reading all his thoughts as they scrolled through his head. She wasn't looking into his eyes, but *through* them, right to his soul.

She finally blinked, looking beyond him to the sidewalk, then back again. Every time her eyes hit his, he felt it like an electrical current. He knew she was trying to decide what to do, and he didn't want to make any move that might turn the tide against him. Her eyes fell closed and she shook her head as she stepped aside.

"Oh, my God. Come in before someone sees us." She glanced down and grimaced. "This isn't exactly my best look."

He closed the door behind him and watched her hurry over to the chair. She picked up the open bag of chips and grabbed paper napkins and a few tissues from the side table.

"Am I the first to discover your neat-as-a-pin persona is all a ruse?"

She turned, her face deep pink. "I was having a pamper-Julie night. So this is…" She looked at all the clutter she had in her hands. "This is an intentional mess. Quinn…what the hell are you doing here?"

"I couldn't stop thinking about what we talked about yesterday."

"You mean, what *you* talked about." Her eye roll was perfectly timed. He wondered if Katie had taught her that trick.

"I may have brought it up, but you didn't shut me down. You said we should be sure, and I want you to know… I'm sure."

Her sharp intake of breath could have been dread or excitement. When she shook her head, his heart dropped.

"I haven't stopped thinking about it, either. But I'm not as sure as you are."

"Okay." He was disappointed, but not surprised. Julie wasn't a risk-taker, and in this case, she might be right. "I just wanted you to know where I stand." She hadn't said *no*, and he could be patient. "Tell me what a pamper-Julie night entails, other than wine and junk food."

She walked into the kitchen, talking over her shoulder as she put away the chips. "It's a girl thing. Soak in a hot bubble bath, slather on some lotion, put on your biggest, softest robe, grab a good book, wine and...junk food." She closed the cupboard door. "Oh, and the most important part? Be alone." She turned to face him, but she wasn't angry. In fact, she looked amused. Sly, crooked smile. Sparkle in her eyes. She propped her hip against the counter and crossed her arms. "And then you showed up." Her smile deepened and she put her hands on the tied belt. "Pamper-Julie night is a very bad night to arrive looking for...whatever you're looking for. I'm wearing multilayered, anti-sex armor."

She tugged the knot loose and let the robe fall open. Beneath the robe, she was wearing pajamas. Cotton ones. With kittens on them. "So instead of exploring our chemistry..." She walked toward the refrigerator. "How about some blueberry pie?"

"No, thanks." If this thing wasn't going to happen, he needed to put some space between them. "I should go. I don't want things to get any weirder than they already are with us."

She retied her robe, shaking her head. "Wow, these pajamas really did chase you off."

"If you think that robe, those chips, or these pajamas are some kind of Quinn-repellant, you are very much mistaken." How could she not know how hot she looked, with her tousled hair and glowing skin?

This was the Julie he wanted, not the one stuffed in a satin gown.

"I gotta go." He turned away, heading for the front door before he embarrassed himself in front of her like some high-school kid.

"Wait!" He stopped, but didn't turn around. Her hand touched his arm. "Quinn...don't go." Her voice was low and uncertain. "I know I said I wasn't as sure as you, but that doesn't mean I want you to go. It's just...you caught me off guard. You know how I hate being unprepared."

He chuckled as he turned around. "I *do* know how much you hate that. So why are you asking me to stay?"

She licked her lips nervously. "I honestly have no idea. Which is part of the problem, right? I have no idea how to do this with any man. You offered to help with that..."

The last thing he wanted to do was talk about *other men* right now. But he had promised to be her adviser, and they'd never set limits on what he could advise on. He reached out and lifted her chin with his fingers. "Are you asking for a sex lesson?"

Her nose wrinkled. "That sounds a little too clinical. I'm not exactly a novice. It's just been a while."

"For me, too."

She ran her fingers up the front of his shirt, and his body responded immediately. He whispered her name and she smiled. It was a sexy, inviting smile. One that looked very, very sure. Her arms slid around his neck, and his hands fell to her waist. She bit her lower lip.

"If you stay, we should have a few ground rules."

"Okay." He understood she needed to feel some sort of control. "Such as…?"

"We are two people trying to find *someone*, but not necessarily each other. So this…whatever happens tonight isn't a commitment to any kind of relationship. And it doesn't have to happen again. We're…exploring. It doesn't mean we're a *thing*, you know what I mean?"

His fingers moved to the knot on her robe and started untying it. Her eyes went nearly black with need. He bowed his head and traced kisses from her chin to her ear, smiling when she trembled.

"Why, Miss Brown," he murmured, "are you asking me for a one-night stand?"

There was the briefest of pauses before she answered. "I guess I am. We can do that, right?"

"As two consenting adults, we can do whatever we want." He brought his mouth back to hers, speaking against her lips. "What do you want, Julie?"

Laughter vibrated through her. "I really hope we don't regret this tomorrow." Her fingers wove through his hair. "But I want you, Qui—"

His kiss silenced her. He'd heard all he needed to hear. He growled as he pulled her closer and took control, plunging into her mouth. Her soft moans

spurred him on. The taste of her drove him wild.
This was a kiss that was going to lead to what he'd
needed from the very first time he'd kissed her. It
was going to lead to *more*.

Julie surrendered to Quinn's kiss without a second thought. He was here in her house. And he
wanted her. For once in her life, she was done being
practical and weighing pros and cons before making a decision. *He wanted her.*

Her robe fell open and he pushed it over her
shoulders to fall to the floor. One obstacle removed,
but she still wore her cringeworthy cotton pajamas.
He pulled back from their kiss and looked down
with an approving smile.

"Very sexy."

She couldn't help but laugh. "You really are hard
up if you think my cat pj's are sexy."

"I'm not looking at the pj's. I'm looking at the
woman wearing them."

A shiver of adrenaline shot through her. She felt
hot, yet somehow goose bumps danced on her body.
They stared at each other as his hands moved under
the pajama top and found skin. His fingertips were
like matches, striking up little flames everywhere
they went.

They stared at each other for a beat, before Quinn
looked around the living room. "Here or the bedroom?"

"Definitely the bedroom. I'm too old for floor sex."

He followed her down the hall. Were they really going to do this? It was one of the most impulsive things she'd ever done, and her heart was practically bursting out of her chest. She made a face when they got to the bedroom.

"Sorry for the mess. This is like the least romantic evening ever. I'm in pajamas, the bed isn't made, there's a pile of laundry to be put away—"

He looked around, his eyebrows gathering together in confusion. "You think *this* is a mess? There's three pairs of socks on the dresser. That's not *laundry*. The bed looks incredibly inviting, and I've already told you what I think of the pajamas." He cupped her face in his hands. "Relax."

He kissed her again. Deeper now. Intense, but not hurried. There was nothing else in the world except the two of them in that moment, surrendering to what now seemed inevitable. His fingers fumbled on the buttons of her top as the kiss continued. Her fingers tugged his shirt free and her hands moved beneath it, sliding up to caress his rock-solid chest. Quinn growled her name as he unbuttoned the last button and pulled open her pajama top. His mouth left hers and he stared at her, his eyes wide with desire.

It was too much for her, and she started to make excuses for herself. "Oh, God, I'm still in my Birkenstocks." She kicked them off. "Pretend these pajamas are silky and sexy, okay?" She'd started to pull the top closed, overwhelmed with an unexpected bout of modesty and embarrassment while facing his gaze.

Quinn gently took her hands, then slid the top back and off her shoulders until it fell to the floor like the robe had. She was barefoot in front of him, wearing only the drawstring bottoms. He looked her up and down, approval etched on his face.

"There isn't any image I could dream up that would make you look any sexier than you do right now." Julie felt her entire body flush. He stepped closer. "You are so beautiful." She started to argue, but his glowering stare stopped her. "Don't you dare start that I'm-not-worthy crap right now. You are *beautiful*. You are *sexy*. I want you so much I can hardly think straight. And I am not going to listen to you diminish yourself. Not now. Not ever."

He brushed his knuckle across her cheek. "You deserve this, Julie. You deserve joy and you deserve passion, and I'm going to do my best to give them to you." He searched her eyes. "If that's what you want."

Her lips were pressed tightly together. She stared at him, and her shoulders slowly began to ease. She nodded. "For the rest of the night, we forget who we are, who we used to be, who we want to be. We're just...us. Here. Now." She paused, glancing down at herself again. "I have one question, though. Why am I one article of clothing away from being naked while you're fully dressed?"

Quinn smiled. "Ma'am, I'm a professional athlete. I can be naked before you get those bottoms off."

Before she could respond, his golf shirt was tossed in the corner, his shoes were off and his hand was on his belt. She snorted, untying her pajamas while he unbuckled his belt. His shorts fell to the floor, revealing dark blue boxer briefs. Never taking their eyes from each other, they finished undressing. Naked in her bedroom with Quinn.

He stepped forward, his hands touching her waist before sliding upward to cup her breasts. She took a deep breath when his thumbs stroked across her peaks. The sensation connected straight from her chest to the apex of her legs, creating a pulsing desire. She did what she'd been longing to do—she ran her fingers through the soft hair on his chest. Then her fingers traced downward across his stomach, then lower still.

She'd barely registered that one of Quinn's hands was tracing down *her* stomach, until it reached the spot that was burning for him. He cupped his hand against her as she wrapped her fingers around him. His other hand was still busy with her breast, making her whole body feel suspended in air as he caressed, pinched and caressed again. He knew just what to do—when to press, when to tease, when to move. It was perfect, and her vision began to go white. She realized she'd stopped moving her hand on him and started to mumble an apology, which he stopped with a kiss.

"It's okay, baby." His head dropped near her shoulder, his words blowing across her skin. "We've got all night. Close your eyes and enjoy the ride."

His head went lower still, until his mouth found her breast. Julie's vision went from white to red as he took her in at the same time his fingers found their mark. She cried out and arched her back. She was nothing but sensation now, and it was only a few seconds before she saw fireworks inside her closed eyes.

She grabbed at his shoulders and held on as tight as she could, calling his name, then giving a startled cry of garbled sound. She was no stranger to orgasms, but what Quinn just did to her was a heck of a lot more than that. Her knees buckled, but he caught her and lifted her into his arms. Her body was still shaking from the impact of what had just happened.

"Easy, sweetheart. I've got you."

Chapter Thirteen

Quinn laid Julie on the bed and crawled over her to look down at her face. Her damp, flushed face. Her golden, unfocused eyes. Her chest rose and fell so quickly he thought she might hyperventilate. She must have had the same fear, because she put her hand over her chest and began to blow out her breaths at a steadier pace. But every few breaths, her chest would hitch as she gasped for air. Her eyes grew clearer, though, and she looked up at him as if he'd just handed her the keys to the universe. He felt a surge of pride.

She reached up and touched his face, her fingers barely brushing his cheeks. "Quinn, that was…wow."

He nodded in agreement. "Very wow."

She frowned. "But you didn't…"

"Trust me, girl. It made me very happy to watch you go."

Her other hand found his hardness and he hissed as she held him. "It's your turn now."

The only sound he could make as she took charge was a muffled curse and a series of escalating grunts until he roared and convulsed at the sweet release.

He collapsed on her with a satisfied sigh. "And… wow again. Holy…everything's a blur. You've wrecked me before we got to the main event."

She giggled, patting his back absently. "The main event? This isn't a boxing ring."

He grabbed her waist, and her laughter increased as he started tickling her. He spoke in an exaggerated announcing voice, as if calling a match.

"And in this corner, ladies and gentlemen, we have Quinn Walker, who managed to ignite his opponent in less than a minute!" Julie was laughing so hard now that the bed was shaking. "Mr. Walker says he had no idea she had such a hair trigger. And in this corner, Miss Julie Brown destroyed Walker using nothing but her hand and a deadly smile. Will there be a rematch…?"

"Yes, please!" Julie shouted through her laughter. "Winner take all!"

Quinn rolled onto his back, clinging to Julie so

that she ended up straddling him. Her bright smile did something weird to his heart. This was yet another side of Julie—uninhibited and happy. It might just be his favorite side of her so far.

"Winner take all, eh?" He reached up to massage her breasts, grinning at the tremor she gave when he touched her. He sat up, holding her in front of him so that she was sitting on his thighs. She locked her ankles behind him. Their faces were inches apart. He cupped her face in his hands. "No *taking*. Nothing but surrender." He kissed her, surprised to feel his desire returning so quickly after what she'd just done to him.

She returned the kiss, which quickly turned from sweet to hot. She was holding his head the way he held hers, both of them trying to exert some control. But this wasn't a competition. He slowed the kiss, running his fingers up and down her back until she was almost purring in his arms.

"Make love to me, Quinn."

She barely whispered the words, but it was all he needed to hear. He gently turned her so that she was back on the bed, with him kneeling between her legs. He had to stretch to reach the condom wrapper he'd tossed on her nightstand. She was determined to help get it on. Her touch was his kryptonite.

He gritted his teeth until the condom was on and he was settling over this woman who'd twisted him in knots. She curled her legs up and over his back, making it easy for him to slide in. They both made similar moans that felt a lot like *finally!* when the connection happened. He paused, just taking in the amazing feel of her. When they started moving, it only got better.

They didn't need words. They just rocked against each other. She nipped his shoulder. He rose up on his knees and went harder. Faster. Her fingernails dug into his back and she moaned his name against his skin. It sounded like a plea, and he was glad for it. They came together without a sound other than their breathing, which stopped for what seemed like a very long time as they clung to each other. He finally lowered her to the mattress, lying on top of her. He was too far gone to move any farther.

"I just need a minute." He mumbled the words into her neck, his eyes closing.

"You and me both." Julie patted his shoulder. She was happy to have his weight and warmth covering her. Without it, she felt as if her body would float right off the bed. Her soul had officially left her body. There was nothing left. Nothing but satisfaction and surprise.

She'd just slept with Quinn Walker. And it. Was. Incredible. It was earthmoving, thunder and lightning, fireworks-finale-with-cannons incredible. With *Quinn Walker.* She brushed her hand up his arm, earning a soft moan in response.

His head moved and he kissed her neck. "You okay?"

She nodded against him. "Very okay. Just trying to wrap my head around what just happened."

His laugh huffed against her skin. "When you figure it out, let me know. Because I have no freakin' clue." He groaned and pushed up on his arms, looking down at her with a smile. "I only know I liked it. A lot."

"*That* we can agree on."

He brushed a strand of hair from her face, his gaze dark and intense. "Glad to hear it. It felt… natural. Very…"

"In the moment? Spontaneous?" She gave him a teasing grin. "That should be right up your alley."

His laughter was warm and quick. "True. How did you feel, just letting go like that?"

"Like you said, it felt natural. And I trusted you."

And there was perhaps the biggest surprise of all. She was able to let herself go with Quinn because she trusted him. Something that didn't come easily for her. He was staring down at her, a strange emotion crossing his face.

"What?"

He smiled, and it extended up to the deep creases at the corners of his eyes. "I'm guessing that's something you don't say a lot." He leaned down and kissed the tip of her nose.

He rolled away and took care of the condom,

then came back to tug her into his arms. Almost as quickly as he did, he was asleep, his breathing deep and steady at her back. Julie stayed awake, wondering what it was about Quinn. He pushed all her buttons, but maybe that was because he was so aware of her. She thought she kept her feelings pretty well under wraps—not only to maintain her professionalism, but also because *feelings* couldn't always be controlled.

Quinn saw right through her guard. He knew when a comment hit her wrong. He knew when she was proud of herself. Heck, he knew when she was sick, just from her texts. He knew she was as attracted to him as he was to her. Had he known she'd never let him leave if he showed up tonight? Probably.

And once they got to the bedroom…oh, he knew her, all right. Every touch, every word, even his jokes—it was all perfect. They were so in sync with each other that it felt effortless. No awkwardness. No doubts. No questions.

"I can feel your brain spinning." Quinn's voice was thick with sleep. "What's on your mind? 'Cuz I gotta be honest, as much as I'd like to, I'm not ready to go again."

Julie snuggled back against him, and his arm tightened around her waist.

"That sex may have exhausted you, but it energized me. I feel like I'm buzzing."

He stretched and yawned. "I'm glad to hear it. You still haven't told me what's on your mind."

"Just replaying our evening. In high definition. With stereo sound."

"Ooh, that sounds like fun." He kissed the back of her neck. "Can I confess something?"

"Sure."

"I know we joked about a one-night stand, but Julie… I want to do this again."

"Again tonight? No problem." She knew that wasn't what he meant. "After tonight?" She turned in his arms so she could look into his eyes. "I don't know. I mean, I want to. I'd be crazy not to want more of that, assuming we can duplicate that level…"

"Oh, I can duplicate it. Maybe even improve on it." He winked and gave her a quick kiss. "So what's the issue?"

"We need to know where this is headed, if anywhere. We need to talk out the plan." She made a face. "Yes, I know that sounds like my usual control freak self, but that's who I am."

Quinn shifted and sat up against the headboard, bringing her with him. She was tucked under his arm, her head on his chest. He thought for a moment. "I know you love plans. But it's hard to *plan* a relationship."

"And now we're in a relationship?" A familiar shiver of doubt hit her. This was where things always went bad—when an official relationship began. She just wasn't built for them, and she always found a way to burn things to the ground.

"Okay," Quinn said. "It's time to tell me what that's all about. Why are you so relationship-phobic? And don't tell me you've just been too busy for the past twenty years. Have you even *tried* to be in any sort of long-term thing with a guy?"

"I've tried, but it's been a while. I told you before, I'm really bad at it. I look for reasons to walk away." She looked up at him. "So consider yourself forewarned."

His hand stroked her arm, calming her with its steady motion. She hadn't even realized how tense she was until he did that. He knew her better than she knew herself, which was a little scary.

"I appreciate the warning, but I'm more interested in the *why* behind it. Did some guy hurt you?" His voice went brittle on those last two words, as if he was ready to do battle if she said yes. If only it was that simple.

"It goes further back than that," she said, emotion rising in her throat. This wasn't a topic she discussed often, but Quinn was genuinely interested, and he deserved to know at least some of the story. "I think I mentioned I didn't have the best childhood."

He went very still. "Did an adult…*do* something to you?"

"Not in the way you're thinking, no." But in oh,

so many other ways. She took a deep breath and told as much as she could. "The adults in my life were…unreliable. My mother was an alcoholic. My dad probably was, too, but he left when I was ten, so it's hard to say. I never saw him after that." She thought of her father, so tall—at least in her childhood memories—and so handsome. He had a big laugh and used to call her his princess. But he'd also had a quick temper, although it had been directed more at her mother than her or Bobby. They generally hid in their bedrooms when things got hot, which was often.

"I'm sorry." Quinn continued to stroke her arm, and she focused on his touch.

"Me, too." Quinn didn't ask for more, but she found herself wanting to talk about it. "Dad was a happy drunk—the life of the party. He'd dance with the women and play poker with the guys. A man's man, you know? Bigger than life." She shrugged. "At least he seemed that way to a little girl. But Mom…" She closed her eyes, pressing closer against Quinn. His grip tightened, but he didn't speak. "Mom was a mean drunk."

It took all her concentration to keep from flinching at the memories. It started with sharp, twisting pinches if she or Bobby didn't get out of her way fast enough, or gave her an answer she thought sounded like "sass." As they got older, the pinches were just the beginning. Mom would slap them. Push them.

Shake them. Her stomach rolled. She couldn't tell Quinn that part. Not tonight.

"Dad kept his drinking to the weekends. He was able to hold down a job, at least until his hot temper got him in trouble. But drinking wasn't an occasional thing with Mom. She was literally the town drunk. Everyone knew who she was, and what kind of home life we had. She couldn't work. Any money she got was spent on booze, not her children. The house was always a mess. People would deliver bags of donated food and clothes for us out of pity."

"Why didn't they try to get you out of there?"

She smiled at the righteous anger in his voice.

"They did. Social Services paid a visit once in a while, so someone must have called and reported her. But back then, it was all about keeping the kids with their mom. She'd cry and promise to get in a program and do better, but it was all an act."

"How did you get through that intact, Julie? I mean…look at you. You're successful and…normal." He sounded amazed. And he hadn't heard the half of it.

She huffed a humorless laugh. "I'm almost forty with fourteen bridesmaid dresses and no wedding gowns. I'm not all that normal."

"I'm just amazed you and Bobby survived that without being…damaged."

"Neither of us is the town drunk, if that's what you mean. But how do you define *damaged*? Neither of us has been able to hang on to a long-term relationship, much less get married. I think we used the experience as motivation to work as hard as we could. We both crave stability more than anything else. Especially me."

"That definitely explains why you like having control over things."

"Doesn't take a psychiatrist to figure that one out, does it?"

"Have you gone to counseling?"

She shook her head. "My school counselor tried to help, but talking about all the ugly details made me feel worse, not better." She knew he'd gone to counseling with Katie, but Quinn accepted her comment without arguing. She relaxed against him, trusting him, at least for now. "And my great-grandmother was a wonderful influence in my teen years. She moved here after Dad left. Mom wouldn't let her live with us, but Nanny got an apartment in town and she gave Bobby and me a safe place to go."

Quinn frowned down at her. "You weren't *safe* at home?"

It felt embarrassing to admit the physical abuse, and even with the trust factor growing between them, she wasn't ready to go there. "Mom was just... volatile—all the time. We never knew what we'd come home to after school. She might be throwing away all our toys in a fit of rage, or she might be painting the living room bright green so we could pretend to live in the forest. Looking back, I'm sure she had some manic tendencies that were more than just booze-related. But drinking elevated it to a whole other level." She tried to give him a smile. "We started going to Nanny's after school for a few hours of tranquility. She's the one who taught me to cook and clean. She encouraged Bobby and me to set goals and go after them. She was the only one outside of school who believed in us and made us see a different sort of future than what we had at home." She paused. "Nanny saved us."

"I take it she's gone now?"

"Nanny? Oh, yeah. She was well into her eighties by the time I graduated high school, and she died not long after that. Bobby and I think she only stayed alive to see us get our diplomas and get out of her granddaughter's house."

"And your mom? Your dad?"

"Mom died fifteen years ago. Drank herself to death, basically. As for my dad, I have no clue. He just vanished from our lives one day. It's like he never existed." He'd promised to come back for Julie. He told her that night that he just needed to find a place somewhere far from Gallant Lake, and then he'd come back and get his princess. But he never did.

Silence stretched between them, but it was a comfortable silence. She'd told her story, and he'd listened with compassion. Finally, he gave her a quick squeeze and turned so she was on her back beside him on the bed. He studied her face.

"That's a pretty good reason to be bad at relationships. But if you overcame your childhood to find success in all the other areas of your life, I'll bet you can overcome it to be in a relationship, too."

"I think that would be a bad bet. I'm a runner. Always have been."

"You're not running now." He had a point. She put her hand on his chest, feeling his heart beating strong and steady. He took the hand and raised it to his lips, kissing her fingers. "I'm not looking for forever. But I like being with you, and I especially like being naked with you. Let's see where it goes." He flashed a grin. "Consider it relationship practice. See how long you can stick."

"And if I can't stick?"

He shrugged. "I've been warned, so whatever happens, we won't be breaking each other's hearts or anything. Like I said, it's practice. No grading. No pressure. Just take it day by day to see where it goes."

"Building relationship muscle memory?" She poked him with her finger playfully, forcing herself to ignore the thought of any broken hearts.

"Something like that." He pushed her back onto the mattress, sliding over her. "Right now I think we need to work some other muscles."

Chapter Fourteen

When Quinn woke in the morning, it took him a minute to figure out where he was. Light was streaming through a window framed with flowered curtains. A soft quilt was draped over the bed. Beneath the quilt, Julie Brown was draped over him. He grinned. Best morning ever. Following the best night ever. The sex had been phenomenal. The conversation had been serious but revealing. And the exhausted sleep they'd both fallen into in the wee hours of the morning had been much needed.

He shifted, doing his best not to disturb her, but ended up disturbing someone else. The cat he'd yet to meet was on the bed and let out a low growl when Quinn stretched his legs. That cat wasn't thinking about pouncing on his feet, was it? He stopped moving, but the cat's attention remained on his right foot under the blanket.

"Don't you dare," he whispered. "Get off the bed. Go on. Get!"

He made the mistake of twitching his foot toward the cat, and it was game over. The pile of white, gold and black fur pounced, using teeth and claws to destroy the intruder in its bed.

"Ow! Goddammit!" Quinn yelled, and Julie snapped awake.

"What?" She followed his glare to find the cat, and damn if she didn't start laughing. "Fluff! Stop that!" She grabbed the quilt and gave it a flick, effectively tossing the cat from the bed to the floor. It meowed in offense, but Julie was still laughing. "I feed you well enough that you don't need to eat Quinn's toes, you bad girl." She looked back to Quinn. "Sorry—Fluff's social skills leave something to be desired, but she and I are stuck with each other."

"Because no one else would want the little terrorist?" He wiggled his foot and winced. "I'm pretty sure she drew blood."

"She's not used to finding a man in my bed." The explanation made Quinn feel better. Julie snuggled against his chest, and he wrapped his arms around her, pulling the quilt back over them. "And you aren't far off the mark as to why she's here. I found her at the entrance to the resort a few years ago—someone must have dropped her off. I gave her to my brother to give to his girlfriend, but Fluff bit her and clawed her sofa to shreds. The cat basically ended their relationship. Bobby was ticked off, so he brought Fluff right back to me and she's been here ever since. We've come to a relative truce. She leaves the furniture alone and I provide food and a litter box. Other than that, we live separate lives. She's usually on my bed in the mornings but vanishes as soon as I wake up." She grinned at him. "She's a grumpy hermit cat."

"And what about you?" He tapped her nose with his finger. "Are you a grumpy hermit?"

She stretched with a sigh. "Only when I'm hungry. And I am starving right now."

He'd had something else in mind, but breakfast wasn't a bad runner-up for sex. They got out of bed and Julie pulled on her robe and went out to the kitchen while Quinn showered and dressed. By the time he got out there, she had a large skillet of eggs, spinach, bacon and cheese coming off the stove. He could get used to this.

They ate in a comfortable silence, then Quinn cleaned the kitchen while Julie went to shower and change. She came back in shorts and a cropped T-shirt, looking refreshed and cheery.

"Does Katie know where you are?" she asked, her eyes wide as if she'd just remembered he had a daughter.

"No, but she stayed with a friend last night. They've had a lot of get-togethers this summer, before they head out into the world to start their college educations."

"Her graduation party is next weekend, right?"

"Yes. Are you coming?" He was having the party at the house. She'd graduated in June, but Katie said she didn't want to compete with her friends' parties, so they'd waited a few weeks. It was going to be casual—basically an open house where people could come and go all afternoon. He'd be grilling hamburgers, hot dogs, chicken and whatever else he could toss over a flame.

She hesitated. "I'd planned on stopping for a little bit, but…now I don't know. Will it be weird?" She smiled. "I guess everything's going to be weird now, won't it?"

He leaned back in the kitchen chair. "It doesn't have to be. I mean, we don't have to announce our relationship at her party, but Katie should be okay with it. She's been pushing me to start dating for months."

Julie's expression turned solemn. "We talked a lot about how I felt about our practice relationship, but…how do *you* feel? Wasn't last night your first time after…?" She couldn't say it. "Was that difficult for you?"

Quinn reached for her hand and held it tight. "There was nothing difficult about last night. Everything about it was wonderful." He swallowed hard, forced to confront his own reason for avoiding relationships. Julie had been open and honest with him during the night, so he owed her the same. "I wasn't thinking of anything but *us* last night—you and me. But…for years, I told myself there'd never be anyone after Anne. You're the first to make me rethink that. Is that a good thing? Probably." He shrugged. "People have been telling me I need to move on for a while now. But I can't help feeling a little like I've betrayed her memory." Julie's face went pale, and he rushed to reassure her. "You did *nothing* wrong. I don't think *I* did anything wrong, either. But this…" He gestured between them. "This was…unexpected."

Julie stared out the window, and he let her process her thoughts.

"Leave it to me," she finally said, almost to herself, "the most insecure person in the history of relationships, to get involved with someone who can't help bringing another woman into the mix. Even if it's a woman who's no longer here."

She wasn't wrong. Anne was in this, whether she should be or not. He gave Julie's hand a squeeze. "It's uncharted territory for both of us. But if we look at this as a trial run, then we can work our way through it a day at a time. No broken hearts, remember?"

She gripped his fingers. "No broken hearts."

* * *

"I wondered if you were going to show up." Amanda greeted Julie at Quinn's lakefront house. She'd had to park up the road and walk because of all the cars. The yard was filled with people, with the high school kids gathered in the front yard with music blaring, and the more mature crowd in back, where the yard sloped to the water. The grills were back here, currently manned by Shane Brannigan and Nick West.

"Why did you think I wouldn't show up?"

"Oh, you know…" Amanda was being coy. "What with you and Quinn doing whatever you're doing."

Julie's eyes searched for him in the clusters of people talking and eating.

"We're not doing anything."

It wasn't a lie. Since Tuesday morning, they'd only seen each other a few times. He was busy preparing for the party, and they agreed it wasn't a good time for him to be telling Katie he was having his own sleepovers. This was Katie's week, and today was her day. But they had managed to squeeze in a few steamy kisses and one very lengthy—and satisfying—make-out session in the golf club's storage room.

She spotted him down near the water, and he saw her at the same time. He lifted his beer in greeting but didn't step away from Jerry and a few other golfers she'd met at the club. It would look suspicious for him to make a big deal of her arrival when they'd been work rivals for so long. At the same time, she felt a sting of disappointment. They'd agreed to keep their new relationship quiet for now, but she couldn't help feeling sidelined.

"Hello?" Amanda waved her hand in front of Julie's face. "Earth to Julie?"

"Sorry. The lake is so pretty here."

"Right," Amanda snorted. "It's not the lake you were admiring. It was the proud papa down there. The guy who's been driving you crazy for three years, and now seems to be driving you crazy in a whole new way."

Blake walked over, handing Julie a plastic cup filled with fruit punch. She sniffed it. Correction—it was sangria. He nodded at the cup.

"Careful, that stuff has a kick to it. I think the kids spiked it without realizing it was already an adult beverage." He gave her a funny look. "So… why are you and Quinn avoiding each other? It's not like you're fooling anyone."

"Why is everyone so convinced there's something going on with Quinn and me?"

"Oh, I don't know." Blake winked at her. "He rescued you when you were sick and spent the night at your place. Then he called in Tuesday morning for a last-minute personal day on the same day that *you'd* taken off. And I saw you trotting over to the golf club yesterday for lunch. You've never had lunch anywhere *near* the golf course."

She could have debated with them, but what was the point? "It's complicated. And new. And this is Katie's graduation party. Today is about her, not a relationship that may never go anywhere. After all, none of my others have."

"Come on," Amanda said, looking concerned. "You're not *that* bad at relationships."

Julie leveled a look at her. "Fourteen bridesmaid dresses."

Her friends didn't have an answer for that. Quinn finally made it over to her, bringing her a plate loaded with food. "This is for both of us. Come sit with me."

They sat at the picnic table near the water. She'd been to the house before, but only to pick up or drop off Katie. It was the opposite of her tiny vintage home in many ways. Quinn's place was very contemporary, with a tall wall of glass facing the lake. Inside, she could see the open floor plan, with circular stairs leading up to the second level. A wide deck stretched across the back, and she imagined the sunset views were spectacular.

"Are you up to stay here tonight?" Quinn's question surprised her. "Katie's been invited to a friend's house."

"Tonight?"

"Yeah. Sorry I didn't give you a heads-up, but

it's been so hectic this week that I forgot until she reminded me this morning." He leaned toward her. "But I'd really like you to stay."

She didn't answer right away.

"What?" Quinn asked. "I can tell you want to say something."

"I can't help thinking…this is your house. Yours and Katie's. Won't it be hard with all the memories and…"

"If you're talking about Anne, she never saw this house. There aren't any ghosts here. Stay with me, Julie. Please."

Once everyone had left and Quinn was cleaning up, Julie found herself wandering among the ghosts he had denied. Everywhere she looked, this house was full of memories. There was a series of posters on one wall from golf tournaments Quinn had played in as a pro, when Anne was alive. A large photograph was framed above the fireplace of Anne and a laughing toddler who was obviously Katie. They were on a beach, splashing together in the foamy waves at the edge of the white sand. Beneath it, a series of smaller pictures lined the mantel. Many were of Katie, but Anne was there, too.

She was beautiful. Katie looked so much like her that Julie wondered how Quinn coped with it. The same strawberry blond curls. The same pale blue eyes and lightly freckled skin. The same bright smile. She looked like she wore her heart on her sleeve, just like Katie did. There was only one photo where she wasn't smiling. She was sleeping in a hospital bed, but the background looked like it was in a family home. Katie, a lanky young teen, was sleeping in the bed with her mother. Anne look thin and frail.

Quinn finished in the kitchen and walked up behind Julie. He stared at the pictures, his eyes troubled.

"Maybe there are more ghosts here than I thought. If you're more comfortable at your place, we can—"

"Tell me about her." Julie was as surprised by her request as Quinn was. "She was a big part of your life. I'd like to know who she was."

He seemed torn, but he finally nodded and led her to the large leather sectional, putting some distance between them and the photos. He told her how shy he'd been as a young man. How outgoing and adventurous Anne had been. How she'd followed him all around to golf tournaments when he was trying to break in to the tour.

He'd proposed to her on her favorite beach, near St. Augustine. They'd honeymooned in Bermuda, spending four days at a beachfront resort there before Quinn played a tournament on the island. A year later, they were parents.

"She was an amazing mom." Quinn glanced at the large portrait of Anne and Katie. "I was just starting to break out on the tour and make good money when she got sick. I golfed during her first round of chemo, flying home whenever I could." He stared out at the lake, shimmering gold in the reflected sunset. "But when the cancer came back… I couldn't do it anymore. I had to be with her and Katie. I came home and stayed home until…"

Julie put her hand on his arm. "That must have been awful for all of you."

"Anne was a hell of a lot stronger than Katie and me. She had a strong faith, and the closer she got to the end, the calmer she seemed to be. She said her biggest regret was leaving us behind."

They sat and watched the sun lower toward Watcher Mountain on the far side of Gallant Lake. It slowly disappeared, throwing even more color into the sky and over the water. Julie wasn't sure what to do now. After that conversation about his late wife, she'd probably managed to make him realize he didn't want Julie to stay. How could she compare with the perfect memories of beautiful Anne? Once the sun and its color palette had changed to the night sky, she stood.

"I'd better get going."

Quinn jumped up, reaching for her. "Why? What did I do?"

She stepped back. "Nothing, Quinn. But…you still love Anne, and you have Katie. This so-called practice relationship is getting complicated."

He didn't argue with a thing she'd said. "I did love Anne very much. But she's been gone for four years. As much as I resisted the idea of dating, I can see now that it's time to…get out there, as Katie keeps telling me. And Katie's off to Tallahassee for school next month." His hands rested on Julie's shoulders and he lowered his head to look straight into her eyes. "I want you to stay with me, Julie. It might feel like the house is full of Anne, but that's for Katie's sake. It's my job to make sure she feels her mother's presence." He turned her around and gave a gentle push toward the stairs. "But *you* don't have to feel it. Come upstairs, and I promise it'll be better."

His suite overlooked the lake, with the bed situated to face the sliding glass doors that led to a narrow balcony. It was very much a man's room, with large-scale, solid oak furniture. An electric fireplace sat in the corner. When he hit the remote, colorful faux flames danced on the screen above the fake logs and glass stones. A wingback chair was near the fireplace, with a stack of magazines and books on the floor next to it. There were stacks of things in a lot of places in his house. She picked up a golf magazine and held it out.

"This issue is six months old. Surely there's a digital version you could read and save a whole bunch of trees." She nudged the stack with her toe, and he shrugged.

"I know. I hang on to them longer than necessary. I'm just worried I'll end up tossing an issue that has an article I might need, for myself or for a student." He looked at the pile of laundry on the floor near the hamper, and the stack of folded T-shirts on his dresser. "I have good intentions, I swear."

She nodded, running her finger along the dusty surface and holding it up for him to see. "Do you *intend* to run a vacuum cleaner up here anytime soon?"

"Oh, ha-ha." He grabbed her finger and wiped it on his shirt, ignoring her protests. "I'm a single dad with a full-time job, and I do the best I can. And frankly, I like my clutter. This is my comfort zone." He raised an eyebrow. "Is that a deal-breaker?"

She looked around. It was more cluttered than she was used to, but, other than a light sheen of dust, it wasn't dirty. And the clutter was organized into piles of like items—printed materials here, clothes there. Oh, and that great big empty bed. No other woman had been in that bed. Her tension eased. In here, there was only Quinn and Julie. She stepped toward him and he opened his arms to embrace her.

"Not a deal-breaker. Perhaps a topic of conversation at some point, but not a deal-breaker. I definitely approve of that large, uncluttered bed over there." He laughed, and the last of their awkwardness was gone.

He grabbed the hem of his shirt and pulled it off

over his head. Julie reached out to touch his chest. She kissed the spot directly over his heart, feeling his pulse beneath her lips. He took her chin and lifted it so he could kiss her, long and deep. The rest of the world fell away beneath her feet. Before she knew it, they were on the bed and their clothes were gone. Their hands traced patterns on each other's skin as they explored in the dark. Then they retraced the routes with their lips. There was a brand-new box of condoms on his nightstand, and they put several of them to very good use as the night went by.

A soft gray predawn light was glowing beyond the windows the final time they came together, whispering each other's names as they held on tight. She was glad Quinn fell asleep shortly after, so he wouldn't see the tears that traced down her cheeks. Her emotions were everywhere when it came to Quinn. He made her feel—body and soul—better than she'd ever felt before.

They kept laughingly calling this a trial relationship, but she had a feeling she might be falling in love with Quinn for real. And that was terrifying.

Chapter Fifteen

"Come on, slowpoke!" Julie ran ahead of Quinn on the trail. She turned and put her hands on her hips like the Jolly Green Giant. "I thought you said you were in shape?"

Quinn straightened and watched her, all perky and smug. She was laughing at him. That was something they'd done a lot together over the last few weeks, whether they were making love, cooking a meal together in her tiny kitchen, or hiking up Gallant Mountain to find the infamous Kissing Rock. This particular adventure was Julie's idea. She'd sprung it on him that morning, after he'd spent the night. She said she was practicing being spontaneous, but when he saw she already had a backpack ready, he called BS on her.

"So are you coming or what?" Julie walked back down the trail to face him. "What are you staring at?"

"I'm staring at *you*." He pulled her in for a quick kiss. "Your cute little behind has been swaying back and forth in front of me all the way up this mountain, and I think it put me in a trance." He'd been enjoying the view very much. "Besides, what's the hurry? It's just a rock."

Her eyes flared open and she put her hand on her chest. "*Just a rock?* Did you not hear me tell you about how popular Kissing Rock is? How for years people have sneaked up the mountain and made out with their sweethearts on the big rock with the great view? It's been happening for generations."

He nodded. "You've told me. At least twenty times since you and Cassie brought it up. I still say it's just a rock."

She waved her hand at him and turned to start climbing again. "Whatever. It's a beautiful spot, and I can't believe you haven't been here yet."

He followed her up the steep path. "I didn't have a sweetheart before now, remember?"

"Well, now you do, so this is a must-see."

They'd been nearly inseparable for the last two weeks. Besides sneaking kisses during the day at work—just because the sneaking was fun—they'd taken the relationship more public. Katie was the first person they told officially, and she'd seemed surprised, but also happy. They'd explained it was a strictly casual, no-labels, just-friends sort of thing. Which Katie hadn't believed any more than their friends did. Everyone seemed convinced that he and Julie made a great match, even if they *had* been battling for three years at work. Their friends kept saying things like *you guys are perfect* and *I knew it!*

He'd noticed his daughter was a little more withdrawn about things if he and Julie were at the house together. She loved going to The Chalet for pizza with them, or to the resort for dinner. The three of them had gone to the llama farm up in the hills outside of Gallant Lake. Katie and Julie had walked ahead of him around the paddocks, laughing together and falling in love with the babies jumping around like they had pogo sticks for legs. The two women had the same sarcastic sense of humor and they seemed to take great pleasure in teasing him about his fashion choices or driving skills. They talked about going skiing together when Katie was home that winter.

But the few times Julie had come to the house for lunch or dinner, Katie had been different. He wasn't sure Julie had even noticed, but he had. Katie was polite and friendly, but he'd caught her at times just watching Julie, looking uncertain. It was as if Julie was fine as a social friend, but bringing her into their house was a step too far. She got a little sharp over simple things like Julie not knowing where the serving spoons were stored in the kitchen. Katie spent even more time than usual rolling her eyes when Julie was there. She was careful that Julie never saw. But Quinn did.

He was letting it go for now. It had been just him and Katie in that house for three years, she was getting ready to head to college and it was all a lot of change for her to deal with. He made sure he and Katie still had their one-on-one time for most meals. Then he'd often go to Julie's house for dessert and… *dessert.* He rarely spent the whole night, because of Katie. He wanted to be home when she got up.

"Ta-da!" They'd reached a small clearing, and Julie was twirling in the tall grass. "We made it!"

The clearing was about the size of the lawn at the resort, surrounded with trees on two sides, a drop-off with expansive views of the valley and lake at the front, and Gallant Mountain anchoring the other end. Getting to the peak would involve rock-climbing skills he didn't possess. At the bottom of the rocky outcrop, though, was a mammoth boulder. It was about the size of a city bus. He nodded toward it.

"The Kissing Rock, I presume?"

"You guessed it." Julie came up to him and

wrapped her arm around his waist. "If you think this view is pretty, wait until you see it from up there."

She led him to the large rock and pointed to where someone had chiseled tiny steps—more like toeholds—into the rock face. They climbed to the top. Once there, Julie instructed him to lean back against the mountain and look out. The rock was just high enough and wide enough that when he stood there, he couldn't see the grassy clearing. He could just see the trees framing a view of Gallant Lake far below. There was the resort. And the golf course. It felt as if they were standing on a cliff overlooking the valley, but they were perfectly safe.

He nodded in approval. "This is pretty cool. It looks like we're flying, or could be if we took a couple steps."

"Isn't it great? You can see the town way down there, past the resort. Straight across the lake is the ski lodge on Watcher Mountain. What a view, right?" Her eyes were bright with happiness. Her hair was in a low ponytail, and her dark knit top and capris were clinging in all the right places. She was glowing.

"Yeah," he agreed, never taking his eyes off her. "What a view."

She must have noticed the intensity in his voice, because she looked over and her eyes narrowed. "I was talking about *that* view, Mr. Flirt."

"I like this view better." He pulled her close, cupping her cheek with his hand and kissing her. She surrendered with a soft sigh, flattening her body against his as the kiss deepened. He didn't think he'd ever get tired of kissing her. It was never the same, but always electric. He turned so her back was against the mountain and he was in front of her, their lips never parting. She hooked one leg around his thigh and he pushed against her, relishing her answering moan.

They didn't part until they heard voices in the trees. She'd said it was a popular spot, so it wasn't exactly a surprise. But it was a huge disappointment. He'd been making plans for a little spontaneous lovemaking on top of the Kissing Rock, but that would have to wait. Two couples stepped into the clearing, laughing and waving when they saw Quinn and Julie on the rock. Yup. He'd been caught red-handed, kissing on a Kissing Rock.

The intruders walked past the rock to continue up the mountain. When they got closer, he noticed their climbing gear. The tallest guy who couldn't be older than seventeen, caught Quinn's eye and gave him an exaggerated wink and two thumbs up. Julie giggled. When the foursome was gone, she nudged Quinn with her elbow.

"The kids seem to think we're doing okay."

Quinn snorted. "They'll probably tell their friends they saw an old couple humping on the Screwing Rock."

She slapped his shoulder. "It's the *Kissing* Rock."

She was in the circle of his arms, looking up at him with so much confidence and affection. Her smile was bright, and she seemed ready to do anything he suggested, just raring to go. And he loved her so damn much.

His heart skipped, stopped, then started again. He was falling in love with her. What was he supposed to *do* with that knowledge? Did she feel the same way? Was he ready to be in love again? What would Katie think? Was it even possible for a guy to fall so head-over-heels in love *twice* in a lifetime?

"What's got you so serious all of a sudden?" She looked worried.

"Let's sit for a minute." They sat on the rock, leaning against the stony mountaintop, legs extended out in front of them, fingers entwined.

"What is it, Quinn?'

"I know we keep calling this relationship *practice* and we tell ourselves and each other that it's supercasual and no big deal. Just a temporary adventure. But…" He lifted her hand and kissed her knuckles. "What if it wasn't?"

Her lips parted in surprise. "But things are going so well. We're having so much fun. Why risk getting into something…heavier?"

"It doesn't need to be heavier. Just more…committed. Something that *isn't* casual. Something real."

Her eyes narrowed on him again. "We both said

we weren't ready to dive in the deep end. I thought we agreed this was a trial relationship?"

She was scared. He understood. He was scared, too. He pulled her onto his lap, staring straight into her eyes.

"Babe, *every* relationship is a trial relationship. They don't all work. There's no shame in that." She started to look away, but he captured her chin with his fingers. "But we can at least commit to *trying*. We keep talking about dating someone someday, but we're dating each *other* right now." He licked his lips, not sure if he could tell her he was falling hard. Not sure if he *should*. "I don't know where we're going, Julie, but I can't think of anything I'd rather do than find out."

Her mouth opened and closed a few times as she struggled with an answer. He figured she was trying to talk herself out of it. Then her hands framed his face and she kissed him. Not a spicy kiss, but not a casual one, either. It was a *serious* kiss, loaded with emotion. Was it goodbye?

"Julie…" He held her tight.

"Shh." She brushed his lips with hers. "I… I'm glad you feel that way. Like it or not, I'm falling for you."

The words moved from her breath to his. He inhaled them, and felt their power course through his veins.

"Oh, I like it. I'm pretty sure I'm falling for you, too."

Her eyes were round and dark, with tiny gold highlights lighting up the sable brown. Burning with desire. But also showing a deep fear.

"It'll be okay, Julie." He kissed her. "We'll be okay."

"I want to believe that, but you don't understand. This is where things always go south for me. I'll panic. I'll look for things to use to put a wedge between us. Any excuse will do. Anything to prove to myself that I can't handle a relationship." Her hands rested on his chest. "I told you—I'm bad at this."

He chuckled. "After last night, I have to disagree. You are very good at this."

"I wasn't talking about that! I'll sabotage this, even if I don't want to. I will."

"What if you just…don't?"

She frowned. "We said no broken hearts, remember?"

"Of course, I remember. But, Julie… I'm falling hard."

She stared for a long time, then slowly shook her head. "You shouldn't."

"Give me a chance to prove you wrong."

Julie put the leftover raspberry pie in Quinn's refrigerator while he put the dishes in the dishwasher. Cassie and Nick sat at the kitchen island, finishing their wine. Blake and Amanda had already left, saying that little Maddy hadn't been feeling well that afternoon. Shane and Mel had gone home, too. Their babysitter couldn't stay late that night. Katie was up in her room.

It was Quinn and Julie's first dinner party as a couple. Her house was too small for a gathering like that, so they'd chosen Quinn's house. The evening had been full of laughter and stories, and she thought it had gone really well. She looked up. All except for Katie.

She'd been standoffish all evening. Julie had done her best to include Katie in the planning, but she'd made it clear she wasn't interested. As their friends began to arrive, Katie had been polite, but not quite friendly. It was completely unlike the outgoing girl who knew everyone at the dinner table so well. Sure, they were a bunch of adults, but they were also friends.

Cassie brought their wineglasses into the kitchen and nudged Julie, her voice a low whisper. "What's up with Katie?"

Julie sighed. "That's the question of the hour." They stepped back toward the pantry while Nick and Quinn talked. "She wanted Quinn to date. She seemed happy when he dated *me* specifically, but I think she's changed her mind."

Cassie squeezed Julie's arm. "Don't let it get to you. It can't be easy to have another woman come into her home. To see her dad with someone other than her mom. She'll get used to it."

"I don't want to bring stress into her life. This is hard enough…"

Cassie's eyes narrowed. "What do you mean? What's hard about you and Quinn?"

Julie started to respond and realized she didn't have an answer. She and Quinn were…easy. Everything they did was relaxed and natural and, on occasion, screaming sexy. It had only been a month or so, but she'd never had a relationship like this. She wasn't suspicious or insecure about things. She wasn't searching for reasons to shut it down. Her love for him came as easily as the rain. All she had to do was tell him.

"You know, I've spent so much time saying I suck at relationships that I don't think I realized that I'm *in* one now, and it's going just fine. It's weird, but in a good way."

Cassie's smile was bright. "I'm so happy for you two. You've brought out the best in each other."

"I think I really do love him."

Cassie wiped a small spot on the countertop, glancing over her shoulder. "Oh, I knew that."

An hour later, she was getting ready to leave. She never stayed at the house if Katie was home, especially with her in whatever mood she was in this week. Julie looked for Quinn and spotted him down on the dock. The long metal dock had a square platform at the end with a bench on it, and Quinn told her he sat there a lot at night, just to soak in the peacefulness of a mountain lake.

Ironically, he'd taken her out in his boat last weekend, and the ride had been anything *but* peaceful. He'd pushed that small jet boat over the water like they were in a race with someone. But once they'd found a quiet cove, he'd dropped anchor and pulled out a picnic basket. They'd spent a couple hours there, eating and swimming and kissing. Like everything else they'd done together, it felt like they'd been a couple forever.

He looked up when she got to the end of the dock and smiled.

"Hi, beautiful."

"Hi, handsome."

She sat next to him on the bench, and they didn't say anything for a few minutes. She rested her head on his shoulder.

"Katie was quiet tonight."

He put his head on hers. "I noticed. She's packing up for school and I think she's more nervous about that than she lets on."

"I think it's me."

He lifted his head and looked down at her. "You think she's upset about us? Something was definitely bugging her tonight, but I don't think it's that."

"You really think she's okay with us seeing each other?"

He brushed a stray strand of hair from her eyes. "If not, she'll get used to it. Why?"

She told herself to protect her heart, but her heart had other ideas.

"Because I'm falling in love with you, Quinn."

He sat up straight, turning to put his arms around her. "Are you serious?"

She couldn't help laughing a little. "Would you prefer I *didn't* love you?"

He laughed, too. "That's a no. I'm just… Julie, I'm falling in love with you, too. And to hear you say it…" He shook his head as if clearing cobwebs. "At the risk of sounding very *un*spontaneous…what do we do now?"

She leaned forward, tracing kisses along his jaw and ending on his lips. "Don't worry. I'm very good at making plans. Are you coming to the house tonight?"

He glanced up at his own house. Katie's bedroom light was off. "Doesn't look like I'll be talking to her tonight. Why don't you head over and I'll be right behind you?" He pulled her to her feet and brought her in for a long, tight embrace. "You have no idea how happy I am right now."

"Me, too." She started walking down the dock. "See you at my place."

She was almost to shore when he called her name. She turned. Even in the darkness, she could see his devilish smile.

"I can't wait to have you say those words to me again. In bed."

She was humming to herself all the way home. She was falling in love. And she felt wonderful. She'd finally found the right guy.

Chapter Sixteen

Quinn stifled a yawn when he walked into his house. The past few nights with Julie had been exhausting in all the best and hottest ways. He didn't think their love life could get any better, but he'd been wrong.

It wasn't just about the sex. They were more at ease. More trusting. More intimate and tender. Their laughter came easier, and when the lights went off, their passion blossomed more quickly than ever. He saw their future stretching out ahead of them, as bright as the sun.

He whistled to himself as he reached into the cupboard for a griddle. He was going to surprise Katie with her favorite blueberry pancakes for breakfast, and then they'd talk. She'd been acting more and more sullen lately. It might be about leaving for college. It might be his increasing absence from home at night. Or it could just be a random bout of teenage angst. But Julie was right when she told him he had to address it. He and Katie would talk it out over the pancakes that she once declared, through a six-year-old gap-toothed grin, the "bestest booberry pancakes in the whole wide world."

He was folding the batter when she came into the kitchen.

"Hey, pumpkin! I'm making your favorite breakfast!"

Instead of returning his smile, she just stared at the bowl of batter in his hands. Her face was pale, and it looked like she'd been crying.

Who the hell had made his little girl cry?

"Katie?" He set the bowl on the counter and walked over to her. Her whole body tensed and she stepped back, avoiding his eyes. A chill settled over him. Someone had hurt his daughter, and he was ready to do battle right here and now. But he had to know what happened first. And whom he had to kill.

"Honey, what is it? What's wrong?"

"You weren't here last night."

He blinked. "Uh…no. Why? What happened?" Had someone come here to the house?

"Were you with Julie instead?" Her voice was

full of accusation, and he had no idea why. A month ago Katie had driven him to Julie's house herself.

"Instead of what?"

Her voice cracked with hurt and anger. "Instead of being here with *me*, Dad."

Quinn's mind raced. What was he missing here? "Honey, were you sick or something? You should have texted. I'd have come right home. You're always first in my book, kiddo."

She jerked back, her eyes dark with emotion and shining with tears.

"Really? I'm *first*? I thought Julie held that spot."

"Are you *jealous* right now? I thought you wanted me to find someone? I thought you liked Julie?" They'd had dinner together at Julie's house a few weeks ago, and the two women had tag-teamed to tease him endlessly about the mess he'd made in her kitchen trying to create a blackened rib roast. "Come on, Kate. Sit down and we'll talk this out over some *booberry* pancakes. There's nothing they can't solve, right?"

"I don't *want* your stupid pancakes, Dad!" Her voice rose. "We don't have pancakes today. We have eggs and hash. Then we watch all the *Bourne* movies and bake a cake and have lasagna for dinner." Her eyes narrowed. "And last night, we *should* have been watching episodes of *How I Met Your Mother* because it was Mom's favorite show. And we *should* have danced to Britney Spears before we went to bed."

Someone *had* hurt his daughter. And that someone was him. Before he could come up with anything to say, Katie poked him hard in the chest with her finger. Just like her mother used to do when she was angry.

"It's Mom's birthday, and you were too busy hooking up with your girlfriend to remember!"

She stormed out of the house, slamming the door so hard he thought the glass might crack. He started after her. She shouldn't be driving in this state. But she turned and went down to the lakeshore instead, stalking out to the bench at the end of the dock and dropping her head in her hands, crying. He stood frozen by the windows. He'd forgotten Anne's birthday.

Every year, he and Katie observed the day as a celebration of everything Anne had loved. Her favorite sitcoms. Her inexplicable love of Jason Bourne movies. Britney Spears music. Poached eggs on corned-beef hash. Lasagna—which they'd never made well, but he and Katie always had fun trying. Then they'd sing "Happy Birthday" after dinner and have cake. Just the way Anne had asked them to do. She wanted them to treat her birthday as a happy day, not a memorial.

Make sure Katie remembers me with joy. Tell her my stories, especially the silly ones.

And he'd forgotten. His stomach rolled and soured as he was filled with self-loathing. He'd forgotten because he'd been busy falling in love with another woman. On Anne's birthday. What kind of husband was he to just…forget? What kind of father would let his daughter down like that? He'd failed them both.

He couldn't do anything about missing the sitcom marathon last night. But he could play catch-up today. He put the pancake batter in the fridge. He had a can of hash in the cupboard, and he dumped it in a frying pan to brown while he poached the eggs and made toast. When it was ready, he plated it, then balanced two empty mugs on the plates while grasping a carafe of coffee in his fingers.

"Dad, I don't wanna…" Katie looked over her shoulder as he approached on the dock, and her eyes went wide. He was pretty sure he saw a hint of amusement in the corner of her mouth, and it sparked some hope that he might pull this off. She started to stand. "What are you doing?"

"Sit. I'm delivering breakfast, and it is *not* pancakes." He handed her a plate of food, grateful he'd made the long downhill walk without dumping it. He joined her on the bench, filling the mugs with coffee. He handed her one and grimaced when he sipped his own.

"Are you drinking coffee with no sugar?" Katie

was hiding that smile again, but it was in there somewhere.

He shrugged. "I was juggling enough without trying to transport *sugar*, too." He pulled silverware from his back pocket and handed it to her. She frowned at her plate.

"This isn't the same, Dad."

"I know, Kate. I'm so sorry. I feel terrible, but we can still make this work." He had to. He owed it to Anne.

Katie stabbed her fork into the hash and took a bite before answering. "It feels wrong to play catch-up. We've done it the same way every year." She took another bite. "This is really good, though."

Quinn felt his chest ease a fraction. "Honey, you'll be off to college in a few weeks. Everything is going to change from now on. Maybe this is Mom's way of telling us that—"

Her fork hit the side of the plate with a clank, her face sour. "Are you trying to say Mom used you screwing some other woman to send us a message? Gross."

"Watch yourself, Katherine." His voice went hard. "I know I made a huge mistake, but Julie Brown is not some random *other woman*. You know her. She's had dinner with us. You can be mad at me. But Julie's done nothing wrong."

Katie rolled her eyes, but a touch of color on her cheeks was evidence he'd made his point.

"Whatever."

They ate in silence for a few minutes.

"You know," he began, "I've always thought Mom would have loved this place." The sun was rising higher, and the lake reflected it in shades of blue, gold and silver on the mirror-smooth surface.

"You've said that at least once a week since we moved here."

"Well, it's true. She loved anything near water, whether it was the beach or a lake or a river. She grew up—"

"In Galena, Illinois, on a river in a Victorian house that her grandparents built. I know Mom's life story, Dad."

He chewed the inside of his lip. Nope—he couldn't let this one go.

"Keep some respect in your voice when you talk about your mother. Especially today, of all days."

Katie set her plate on the bench and stood. "That's rich—you telling me to respect Mom on the birthday you forgot."

"I said I was sorry. It was a mistake."

"You were distracted with your *girlfriend*."

He stood to face her. He was already mad at himself, and Katie was just feeding that fire. "*You're* the one who's been pushing me for months to start dating again. Which is it, Katie—do you want me to date or not?"

Her eyes filled with tears. "I want you to remember my mother!" She nearly screamed the words at him. "I never thought you'd just move on as if she never happened. You keep saying she'd love it here, but she sure as *hell* wouldn't love what you're doing with Julie."

He took her arms, waiting until she was glaring straight up at him.

"I wouldn't be doing this if she was here." His voice cracked, thick with the emotion that was nearly choking him. "If your mother was here, I'd be loving *her*. Hell, I'll *always* be loving her—until the day I die. I'll never love anyone the way I loved her, Katie. I'm sorry I hurt you today, but you know Anne was the love of my life." He swallowed hard, trying to control the sense of loss welling up inside him. "There will never be anyone else like her for me. *Never*."

There was the tiniest of sounds from the shore. A brief, strangled gasp of pain. Quinn looked up and saw Julie standing there, his jacket in her hand. The color had drained from her face. Her lips parted as if she'd absorbed a blow. From him.

He breathed her name, and she shook her head sharply. His heart had been torn open by his daughter's disappointment in him and his own guilt. But Julie's expression was what destroyed it.

She blinked a few times, then shook her head again. Her whole body shuddered, but Quinn couldn't move. He released Katie, who was wide-eyed with an unreadable emotion. Julie swayed, then seemed to regain control, her expression changing from grief to cool detachment.

"You forgot your golf jacket. I thought you might want it."

The jacket fell from her fingers, landing on the grass in a bright blue mound. She turned and walked up toward the house without another word. Her movement was as robotic as her voice had been.

Quinn was faced with an impossible choice. Letting his distraught daughter believe he wanted to forget her mother, or allowing the second woman he'd ever loved walk out of his life without a fight. He stayed on the dock and watched Julie leave. Right now, Katie came first. But when he looked at her, there was even *more* disapproval on her face.

"You're letting her go?"

"I'm not going to leave you standing here, thinking I was abandoning you or your mother's memory." He'd done the right thing, but the pain was finally hitting him. Julie's departure had been like a razor cut, where the pain doesn't come instantly, but when it does, it's deep and shattering. He had to be a father right now. But the man in him was curled up in howling anguish. He pushed past it to speak.

"Katie, your mom's not here, but she's still part of every breath I take." He tugged her close, then wrapped his arms around her and kissed her forehead. "I forgot a date on the calendar, honey. I did *not* forget her."

"Okay." She buried her face in his shirt. He wasn't sure what *okay* meant, but at least she didn't sound angry anymore. They stood there for a minute, his head resting on hers. His beautiful girl. The best parts of him and Anne were in Katie. He'd do anything to protect her and keep her happy, no matter how much it broke his heart.

Katie pulled her head back to look at him. "I believe you when you say how much you loved Mom. It *was* just a date, and I could have reminded you but I didn't."

"So you were testing me."

"Maybe. Everything is changing, and I... I'm leaving..." He started to protest, but she talked over him. "I know—we'll still see each other and I'll be home in the summertime, but it won't be the same. Nothing will ever be the same."

He brushed a tear from her cheek with his thumb. "Your mom liked to say that life moved in circles, or seasons. That when one season ended, another was waiting right there to take its place." He grinned. "She said it a lot about you growing up. The baby season had its joys and challenges, and then it was gone. And you became a toddler, and that had its own joys and challenges. And then you were a little girl heading to kindergarten. Anne said each season was meant to be. Leaving one season behind was scary and hard, but each new season was a blessing. It was just the way life worked." He caught another tear on her face, and Katie gave him a trembling smile.

"I remember. Are you saying I'm changing seasons? Going from high school to college?"

"More like going from teenager to young adult. From home to the world. It's one of the biggest transitions you'll ever have. It's normal to be scared."

"But, Dad, you're transitioning, too. From being a dad to…being a bachelor." She looked up toward the house, where Julie had walked away.

"Maybe," he conceded, ignoring the screaming voice in his head telling him to run after Julie as fast as he could. "But maybe losing my little girl to the big wide world is enough change for your old dad right now."

Katie stepped back and studied him. Her back was straighter, and her tears had stopped. "You were right when you said Julie didn't do anything wrong. I'm sorry. I was just so mad. You should go talk to her."

How could he convince Julie of anything when he was suddenly unsure?

"Talking about your mom reminded me that I had the most amazing love story with her. Would it be fair to Julie to try to love her when I know I still love Anne?" Katie didn't answer. He didn't expect her to. She had no experience at love, and he'd been a pretty bad example to follow. "I need to think things through before I make any decisions, for everyone's sake."

Especially Julie's. She deserved more than a man who didn't know if he could love her enough.

"Hey, Jules, do you have any extra…?" Cassie stopped short at the entrance of Julie's small office. "What happened?"

Julie tried to smile as if nothing was wrong, but it felt more like a grimace, and must have looked like one, too. Cassie stepped inside and closed the door behind her. "Are you sick? Are you hurt? Do I need to go hurt someone for you?" Her eyes narrowed. "What did Quinn do?"

"I don't want to talk…" She gasped in a breath, trying to catch the sob in her throat. "I just want to be alone, Cass. Really."

Cassie's look of compassion nearly did Julie in completely. Cassie pulled her phone from her pocket and started typing. At the same time, she grabbed Julie's purse from a file cabinet and tossed it at her.

"A resort full of people is *not* a good place to be alone. And being alone-alone is not what you need, anyway. That's the path to self-pity. You need friends. Stat. Come on." She glanced at her phone when it chirped. "Amanda's expecting us at Halcyon."

Julie was too numb to argue. She followed Cassie

out the back entrance of the resort. They walked up a winding trail into the trees and through an old iron gate that led to a spacious manicured lawn. It rose gently from the lake to the pink granite mansion. A wide circular veranda was framed with climbing roses. The only thing missing from the fairy-tale setting was a damsel in distress and a white knight riding up to save her.

Instead, Amanda was standing on the veranda waving a bottle of wine and clutching several long-stemmed wineglasses in her other hand.

"Come on up! Zach's mowing lawns down at the resort this afternoon and I just dropped Maddy at a sleepover with one of her little friends. Halcyon is blessedly empty of children and husbands." They climbed the stone steps to the veranda and sat at the glass-topped iron table. Amanda raised the umbrella to provide shade and started pouring wine. "Mack is bringing a couple more bottles for us, and she's going to pick up Brittany and Mel." Mackenzie Adams owned the liquor store in town, and Brittany was a local real estate agent. They'd both married local guys.

"You don't have to do this…" As good as the wine tasted, Julie couldn't help thinking she just wanted to be home with her cat and her broken heart.

Amanda sat and stared at her in disbelief. "You are my *best* friend. Of course, we have to do this.

Gallant Lake women stick together." She winked. "And this way you'll only have to tell the story once."

There was some logic to that argument. She didn't want to have to repeat to everyone that she and Quinn were done. And just like that, the tears came again. She'd have thought there couldn't be any more left inside of her after crying all the way to work, then hiding in her office and crying some more.

Within minutes, Mel, Mack, Brittany *and* Nora had joined them. Mack tossed her thick mane of blond hair out of her face and set three bottles of what Julie knew was very expensive wine on the table.

"We grabbed Nora right off the sidewalk." Mack laughed. "Jillie would be here, too, but she and Matt drove up to Lake Placid for a few days. Matt's never seen it without snow." Her smile faded as she took a seat next to Julie. "This is every available member of the squad. What's the emer—" She looked at Julie's tear-streaked face and froze. "What happened?"

It was a perfect early-August day. The sun was playing hide-and-seek behind puffy white clouds. The lake was bright blue, with small waves lapping at the shoreline. A gentle breeze kept everyone comfortable despite the warm temperature. Julie closed her eyes and soaked it in, remembering that, just like when she was a child, the world was going to keep on spinning no matter what happened in her life. Her friends waited in silence. They were there for support. And as much as it galled her to admit it, Julie could use that right now.

"I overheard Quinn—he and Katie were arguing…over *me*, I guess." She told them how devastated Katie seemed to be, how furious she was with Quinn for having someone new in his life. How it was the opposite of what Katie told Julie before, when she'd seemed eager to see her dad start dating.

Nora interrupted. "What kids *think* they want their parents to do and what they *actually* want their parents to do are often very different things. Trust me. Even when they're grown up and on their own, seeing a parent with someone else is…complicated."

Mack nodded. "Chloe's a lot younger than Katie, of course, but she had her moments when Dan and I started seeing each other. On one hand, she liked me and her dad was happy. On the other, her dad was spending time and affection on *me*, and she had to get used to that."

"I think I could have handled Katie's feelings about it," Julie said. "We could have at least talked about it. But Quinn told her that Anne was the love of his life."

There were murmurs of understanding around the table, and Julie told them how Quinn had been very adamant with Katie that he'd love Anne until the day he died. That he'd never get over her, no matter how long he lived. That he'd never love anyone the way he loved her. *Never.*

After a beat of silence, Nora spoke again. "Grief is a difficult thing to navigate, Julie. Asher was nearly out of his mind with it when I met him. He had lost a child and was terrified of loving his own grandson because he might lose him, too. It made him do things that pushed people away, but that didn't mean he didn't still need and love those people." She smiled. "Including me."

"Remember how wrecked Blake and Zach were when I met them?" Amanda asked. "Blake had lost his sister. Zach had lost his mom and become the ward of an uncle he barely knew. They both lashed out in their grief. It happens."

Julie pulled her hand away. "I know how grief works, ladies. But this is a man grieving for a *woman*, not kids or parents or siblings. The mother of his child. A woman he laughed with and slept with and called his soul mate. He said he'll never love anyone else like he loved her. But a few days ago he said he loved *me*. So which is true?"

"Maybe you need to ask *him*." Brittany, ever the straight-to-the-point sort of woman, said. "Maybe he was just saying what Katie needed to hear. If he didn't know you were there—"

"He knew. Right after he said it, he looked straight at me."

The raw pain on his face had made her take a step back. His eyes had been swimming in it.

Mel leaned forward. "We all know men can be idiots. Did he at least try to fix it?"

Julie shook her head slowly. "Nope. I'd stopped at his place to drop off his jacket, and I saw them out on the dock. I heard every word. I left the jacket." Dropped it to the ground, actually. "Then I walked away and he didn't say or do a thing."

"Ouch," Mel answered. "I know he was with Katie, but…"

"If he and his daughter were arguing," Nora said, "he might not have been able to walk away. Give him a chance to reach out, Julie. I know he cares about you."

"*Caring* about me and *loving* me are two different things." How many times had people—counselors, teachers, family—told her that her parents *cared about her.* She wasn't going to settle for that. "I'm not upset that he loved his wife. I'm happy he did. But I've been an afterthought in every important relationship I've ever had. If I can't be The One for a man, then what's the point?" She drained her wineglass. "I may as well stay single and get more cats."

Amanda laughed softly. "I think Fluff might have opinions about that. All I ask is that you give him a chance to explain."

There was no way to explain away the hurt of knowing he'd never love her enough.

"Maybe. But not tonight. I really just want to eat something…" The wine had hit her empty stomach hard. "Get some sleep and try to forget today ever happened."

"That sounds like a reasonable plan." Mack refilled wineglasses. "Rest never hurt anyone."

"We keep drinking this much," Amanda chuckled, "and you'll *all* be having a sleepover at Halcyon."

Mel promised to deliver everyone safely home, since she and Brittany were drinking sparkling water instead of wine. Brittany was pregnant and Mel was a recovering alcoholic.

Quinn was sitting on Julie's front steps when Mel stopped in front of her house. Brittany was the only one left to be dropped off after Julie, and she gasped when she saw him. "Do you want to come home with me instead? I could have Nate come over and send him on his way…"

"No. It's okay. May as well get this over with." Doing it without all this wine in her system would probably be smarter, but then again, maybe the alcohol would give her the courage she needed.

Quinn stood and watched Mel drive away. "Did your car break down?"

"Nope." She had a little trouble getting the key in the lock, and amusement crept into his voice.

"Had a bit to drink?"

She didn't like the image that came into her

mind. The image of her mother arriving home swaying on her feet after a night of drinking. Her voice hardened. "You do not have any business asking that question."

"I… Okay," he conceded. "Fair enough."

Fluff welcomed them—if anyone considered screaming for food as if she'd been left for days to be a welcome. Julie walked into the kitchen to get some cat food, and Quinn followed, closing the front door behind him.

"Why are you here, Quinn?"

"You know why." He looked into her eyes, then blinked away. "I'm sorry for what you heard earlier."

"Sorry I heard it?" Her snark was definitely fueled by the wine. She wasn't going to play nice tonight.

He jammed his fingers into his hair, then locked his hands together at the top of his head. "This whole day has been such a muck-up. Katie and I always celebrate Anne's birthday together and make it a big thing. A way to keep her alive for Katie, you know? And…I forgot."

Julie couldn't help feeling a stab of sympathy. It certainly explained why Katie was so angry with him. He dropped his hands, staring at her with sorrow and guilt in his eyes.

"I forgot her, Julie. And… I can't do that. I can't let Anne just disappear. I *loved* her."

She raised both hands to stop him. The feelings

he was expressing were normal and he had every right to them, but they were like daggers to her.

"I am not the one to be having this conversation with. You should leave."

"Let me explain—" He took a step, but she backed away from him. If he touched her, she'd lose her resolve. It hurt him. She could see it in his face. But dammit, *she* was hurting, too.

"Think about what you're doing. You're explaining to *me*—the woman you recently declared your love to—how much you're still in love with your dead wife. I am *not* ready to listen to this. Not tonight."

She'd trusted him with her heart, and he was making her feel like an *also-ran*.

"I get it. I do. But I love you, too." He winced when the words came out. "That didn't sound right—"

"I think it sounded exactly right." She felt the walls coming up around her heart like an iron fortress, protecting it the way she'd done her entire life. From her father's betrayal. From her mother's dismissal. From all the mocking words tossed at her. By them. By her schoolmates. By the social worker who'd believed her mother's lies. "You don't love me enough if you have to add a *too* after the words. I've been a runner-up enough in my life, Quinn. I'm not going to be a runner-up in love."

"That's not what I was saying."

"But it *is* exactly what you said. Not only tonight,

but this morning on the dock. You'll never love anyone like you loved Anne." Her emotions settled into
a cold hard ball where her open heart used to be.
"That doesn't leave enough for me."

"Oh, come on," he said, frustration as clear in his
voice as it was in his narrowing eyes. "I was trying
to reassure my daughter. She was upset, and I…"

"So what you said wasn't true?"

"No. I mean…yes, but…" He stared at her, then
shook his head. "I don't know what you want me
to say. I'm not going to apologize for loving her
mother. For wishing Anne hadn't died. You wouldn't
want me to, would you?"

Silence hung in the air between them.

"No. And you wouldn't want *me* to always feel
like second best, would you?"

"Of course not." The anger faded from his voice,
and resignation set in. "I thought I knew where my
heart was, but forgetting Anne's birthday rattled me
as much as it did Katie."

"I'm sorry that happened. But we can't move forward when you're not sure where I fit in your life."

His face went pale.

"I'm sure I love you."

She took a deep breath, a sad sense of certainty
growing. "I don't think you love me *enough*." And
that was exactly the problem. "I've had lots of experience not being loved enough. I don't need another one. I'm tempted to tell you I'll love enough

for both of us, but that's what I've done my whole life, Quinn." She lifted her chin. "I deserve more."

He stared at her, looking broken.

"You're right. You *do* deserve more." His shoulders dropped in defeat, and he turned to go. The fact that he didn't even try to fight told her she'd been right to stand firm. But, oh, how she'd *wanted* him to fight. To fight for them. To fight for her. Instead, he said a quiet good-night and left.

The iron fortress in her chest was empty. Her heart had left with Quinn.

Chapter Seventeen

"What the hell did you do?" Blake Randall marched into Quinn's office just before noon, and he was not happy. Nick West was hot on his heels. *Perfect.*

"What?" Quinn spread his hands, figuring Blake was mad about him taking a day off earlier in the week to be with Katie for Anne's birthday. Things had gotten off to a very rough start with the argument, but they'd watched Anne's favorite movies together and some of the tension had eased. And then Julie had broken his heart. "I had a personal day coming. Jerry covered for me here. There were no problems that I know of."

"No problems, eh?" Blake basically threw himself into a chair across from Quinn. Nick grabbed another chair and spun it so he could straddle it and give Quinn the stink eye as Blake kept going. "How about the problem of me not having a resort manager for two days now? How about the problem of my wife and her pals getting day-drunk with your girlfriend at my house? How about your girlfriend crying on his wife's shoulder—" Blake pointed at Nick "—and telling her she's going to die a lonely old cat lady?"

"Julie hasn't been to work?" His plan had been to give her time before they talked again because… well, because he didn't *have* a plan.

"Oh, she showed up yesterday," Nick said. "Red-eyed and crying. She locked herself in her office until Cassie went in and got a look at her. Then it was Girls Gone Wine all afternoon and now everyone's pissy. Cassie came home and lit into me for 'being such a man.'"

Blake nodded grimly. "Amanda brought up the fight we had when we were just getting started years ago. Nate said Brittany was the same way, telling him if he loved her, he'd trust her or some nonsense." His heavy eyebrows lowered. "The common denominator is Julie and *you*."

"You guys are mad at *me* because *your* wives gave you some grief last night? That's not on me."

"Dammit, man." Blake lowered his head into his hands. "This is why I warned against you and Julie getting involved unless you were serious. I told you to go somewhere else if you were just scratching an itch, because she deserves more than that." He looked up. "And because I need you *both* on the job."

Nick leaned forward, not looking anywhere near as angry as Blake. In fact, he looked amused. "How did you screw things up so badly?"

"She heard me talking to Katie…*arguing* with Katie." He'd barely slept since then, so it was all a little foggy. "I was telling Katie how much I loved her mother. How Anne was the love of my life, and I'd never love anyone again like that…"

Both men were staring at him now, eyes wide.

Blake held his hand up, pinching his fingers together as if trying to grasp a thought. "Let me get this straight. You've been seeing Julie and things were getting serious between you two. And then she heard you talking about never loving anyone like you loved your first wife. Is that what happened?"

"More importantly," Nick added, "what did you say to her once you knew she heard it?"

"I went to her place last night, but she…wasn't very receptive. She's hurt and angry, so I figure I should just leave her alone for a while."

"So," Nick began, "you *want* her to leave you? You want her to think you couldn't love her as much as you loved your wife?"

Blake stared at Quinn. "Because *you're* not sure you can."

Quinn blew out a long sigh. "Because I'm not sure I *should*."

After a long pause, Blake quietly tapped something onto his phone. Saying the words out loud had reopened something in Quinn. It was a wound he'd buried after Julie walked away. He leaned back in his chair, covering his face and swearing bitterly.

"I told you, Blake. I've *had* my true love. What made me think I deserved to have *two* of them? What if I can't love Julie the way she *needs* to be loved? What if—"

A female voice stopped him. "You weren't kidding, honey." His eyes snapped open to see Amanda standing in his doorway. "He's a hot mess." Cassie peeked over Amanda's shoulder into the room, waving brightly at Quinn.

He looked between Blake and Nick. "You called your *wives* on me?"

"I thought you just did something stupid." Blake pulled Amanda onto his lap and kissed her. "I have experience at fixing *that*."

Nick nodded, turning his chair around and offering it to Cassie. He stood behind her, hands on her shoulders. "Stupid things can be fixed," he said, "but this is a job for better minds than ours."

"How is she?" Quinn asked Amanda. The thought of Julie hurting so bad she couldn't go to work made him feel ill. Amanda gave him a thin smile.

"She'll be fine. With or without you. The people who care about her will make sure of it, despite what you've done."

"Easy, tiger," Blake chuckled. "We're trying to fix this, not banish Quinn from the kingdom."

Amanda's eyes narrowed on Quinn. "If you can't even figure out how much you love her, then you don't deserve her."

"I know that, dammit!" He scrubbed the back of his neck. "That's what you're all missing here. I'm not good enough for her! The whole reason you're here is because I hurt her."

"You're making this way too complicated." Amanda's voice softened, and so did her gaze. Her pity was harder to take than her anger. "Julie *loves* you, you knucklehead. All you have to do is love her back. That's it."

"Oh, really? That's it, huh? All the problems will be solved if I just love her? What about Anne? What about my daughter? What about—"

"I'm not saying love *solves* it all. But love will get you *through* it all." Amanda leaned forward, Blake's arm holding her securely. "And being loved is more than Julie Brown has *ever* gotten in return from anyone she opened herself up to. She didn't just open herself up to you—she put her heart out there. She fell in love with you and, more importantly, she *trusted* you with that love. And you're thinking about just…walking away? You will crush her."

Quinn flinched, feeling the pain himself.

Cassie sounded as disappointed as Amanda, but her voice was firm. "But we'll make sure she survives it. Survives *you*."

"That's not what I want." He stared up at the ceiling. "I don't want her hurting. I don't want her just *surviving*. I want her to be happy. To be loved the way she deserves."

"Then act like it." Amanda made it sound so simple. "Love her the way she deserves."

"What if it's too late?"

Blake huffed out a low laugh. "You think she fell out of love with you in a day and a half? That doesn't sound like the Julie I know."

"But you might have to work for it," Nick said, and he, Blake, Amanda and Cassie all laughed.

"How is that *funny*?"

"Because we've all been there." Cassie smiled, looking up at Nick and patting his hand on her shoulder. "And we've all made it through by loving each other."

"And groveling," Nick added, making Cassie giggle. "Lots and lots of groveling."

"First," Blake cautioned, "you need to figure out where your head is at. Because if you're really not sure, don't drag out the hurt. But if there's any chance you really love that woman, don't lose her."

Quinn blinked.

"I *do* love her."

His four guests—advisers…*friends*—all relaxed at his words.

"About time you realized what we've known all along." Blake smiled.

"I still need to talk to Katie. This isn't about just Julie and me."

Cassie and Amanda looked at each other.

"We'll handle Katie," Amanda said.

Quinn couldn't help laughing. "I'm afraid to ask what that means."

"It means sometimes a woman needs to hear things from other women," she answered. "Katie's mom isn't here to help her navigate life's challenges from a woman's perspective. But she has a circle of moms in this town who can guide her."

"Which means," Blake said, giving Quinn a pointed look, "that all you have to worry about is Julie."

Worrying about Julie was an all-consuming task right now. Hating the hurt he'd caused. Grieving the life together that might not happen. The idea of loving someone again after Anne was terrifying.

But not as terrifying as the thought of a life without Julie in it.

"Try to sell it at least a *little*, girlfriend." Luis Alvarado gestured for Julie to take another spin on the make-believe runway in the upstairs design center at Five and Design. It was one of the last rehearsals before the charity weekend, and she'd been foolish enough to agree to model one of the dresses herself at the show. Today she was wearing the actual dress for the first time.

"Sorry, Luis. I'm way out of my comfort zone here. Is it the walk that needs work?"

"Your walk is fine. It's your face I'm worried about."

"Luis!" Mel scolded from the table where she was putting together brochures. "Mind your manners."

"I didn't mean her actual face." He looked at Julie. "I'm sorry. I meant your expression. I forget I'm not working with professional models here. They're used to my rehearsal moods. The dress is kick-ass, but you look...*not* kick-ass."

"He's got a point." Mel walked over and assessed Julie.

This. This was why she hated being the center of attention. The judgment, even coming innocently from friends, was excruciating. She was okay when she was dealing with employees or guests—there was an invisible wall there between her feelings and their opinions. She knew what she was doing on the job, and that certainty kept the wall firmly in place. Not that she didn't care, but she could deflect any negative opinions so they didn't dig in.

"This was a bad idea..."

"Come with me," Mel said, leading Julie to a

bank of floor-length mirrors in the back of the room. "Look in that mirror. What do you see?"

"A beautiful dress."

It was true. Luis had taken the bejeweled band from the neckline of the hot pink gown and combined it with the black sheath, now minus its ostrich feathers. The crystals ran diagonally from one shoulder down to Julie's hip, meeting the newly added slit in the skirt. When she moved, the bright pink satin, which now lined the skirt, flashed provocatively. Two outdated dresses had become trendy and elegant as one.

She raised her chin as she appraised her reflection. The dress fit perfectly, hugging her figure while still leaving room for her to move and breathe.

"What do you see besides the dress?" Mel asked.

Julie stared, then cringed when she realized what Luis had been saying. Her face was pale and sad. Tired.

"I see a woman who needs a lot more sleep and a lot more makeup." She sighed. "Why didn't you tell me I looked like death warmed over? There's no way I can model this dress next week."

"Sweetie, this dress is a couture gown made specifically for you. Meaning no one else can wear it." Mel held Julie's shoulders from behind, resting her chin on her shoulder and looking into the mirror. "And the issue isn't the makeup. Like Luis said, it's your expression. You look like you can't decide if you need to take a nap, have a drink or commit a murder." She gave her a gentle shake. "You're gonna get through this, Jules."

She nodded, unconvinced, but repeating the words anyway. "I'm gonna get through this."

Mel straightened, patting her back. "And you may as well start now."

It had been three days since everything had fallen apart with Quinn. Since he'd promised a distraught Katie that he would never love Julie as much as he'd loved Anne. That he'd never stop loving Anne at all. Even worse, he hadn't reacted when he saw Julie standing there, knowing she'd heard everything. He'd let her walk away.

Yes, he'd come to the house that night to claim he loved her. But when she said she wasn't sure he loved her *enough*, he hadn't answered. And he'd agreed that she deserved more. More than him. When he was the only one she wanted.

He'd called once since then, but she told him she wasn't ready to talk. Yesterday, he'd left a long, rambling voice mail saying how sorry he was. How he was doing his best to figure out what was right for everyone. She hadn't returned the call. There was no point talking until he got his head together.

"Julie?" Mel's voice made her flinch.

"What?" She couldn't even remember what Mel was saying. She really did need to get some sleep.

"I *said*, you're going to get through this. And

you may as well start right now." Mel tsk-tsked at her. "Come on, let's get you out of that dress. It's impossible to get salt out of satin."

It took a moment for Julie to realize Mel was talking about the tears on her face. They carefully removed the dress and she changed into her usual work attire—slacks and a polo shirt under a light-weight jacket.

"Sometimes people need to walk right into their mistakes and wallow there for a while before they realize what's going on." Julie knew Mel had gone through something similar with Shane. "They hang on to old identities and fears because that's the only territory they know. The smart ones figure it out eventually, and rewind so they can take a differ-ent path." Mel draped a plastic bag over the gown to protect it, tagging it and setting it on the rack of repurposed clothes for the Sustainable Style show. "It's a lot like these clothes. They start as one thing, but get a second chance to be something fresher and—" she glanced sideways at Julie "—more joy-ful."

Mel and Luis had outdone themselves for the fashion show this year. Some secondhand conver-sions were more for inspiration than practicality, like Julie's couture two-in-one evening gown. But many of the styles were things anyone with sewing skills and a little imagination could tackle. From jeans made into floor-sweeping denim skirts embroidered with sparkling threads, to 1990s wool blazers converted into handbags with leather trim.

Julie stared into her own eyes in the mirror and ran a brush through her hair, finally turning to face Mel. "Are you talking about Quinn or me?"

Mel's cheeks turned pink. "As Prince Charming once said...*if the shoe fits*." She winked. "But I was actually thinking of Quinn. Give him a little time to figure things out. But that doesn't mean you have to stand still and wait. Because if he *doesn't* free himself from all that wallowing, then you're going to have to move on." Mel gave Julie a quick, tight hug, then held her out at arm's length. "I'm not saying don't be sad, but don't be sad *all* the time. You have a job and a life here, and you are going to be *fine*. Got it?"

Mel was right. The upcoming Travis Foundation weekend was important to the community and to the veterans it helped. And Julie needed to snap out of her doldrums and make sure it was a success. She headed back to the resort and straight to the whiteboard in the staff room, otherwise known as the charity weekend planning hub. She looked at her own lengthy checklist of things to inspect before the weekend.

Halfway down the list, she saw a note to check the setup at the golf club before Friday's cocktail hour. She dismissed the tightness that crept up her spine. Like it or not, she and Quinn worked together. Luckily, there was no need for them to see each other every day, or even every week, except for a few months during the summer when tournaments required their cooperation. No doubt, this first event would be the toughest, but she was sure they'd get used to setting aside their personal feelings and getting the job done. She didn't *hate* the man. They'd tried a trial relationship and it didn't work. The only rule they broke was the one about no broken hearts.

She knew the plaid tablecloths had arrived—each a different color combination and pattern. The centerpieces would be silly stuffed woodchucks wearing golf visors, sitting in a shallow vase of colorful carnations, each arrangement dyed to match the individual tablecloths. Guests had been invited to wear their worst-matching plaids and patterns for the cocktail party. It had been Quinn's idea to have a *Caddyshack*-themed event. It would be silly and fun and nothing at all like the formal party she'd originally envisioned.

She waited until Thursday to go inspect everything at the golf club. Even though the party was on Quinn's turf, it was technically a resort event, which meant she was responsible. Dario would take care of all the food and drinks, but she couldn't assume Quinn would know how to plan a cocktail party that would be attended by celebrities and other wealthy donors to the foundation. That was her job. With any luck, he'd be busy doing something out on the golf co—

"Julie?"

No such luck. She turned to face Quinn. There was some consolation in the fact that he looked just as exhausted as she did. The lines around his eyes were deeper than ever. There was a grayish pallor under his tan that said he wasn't getting much sleep. But there was a heat in his eyes that warmed her from the inside out. He wanted to touch her. Kiss her. She could see it not only in his eyes, but also in the way he stood, alert and totally focused on her. He was fighting it. Controlling himself. Which was more than she could say for the riot going on in her heart right now.

Run to him! She didn't move. *Run to him!* No. They'd both agreed she deserved more than he could offer. *Run to him!*

"No!"

Julie gasped, realizing she'd said that out loud. It was a whisper, but a loud one. Quinn misunderstood, stepping back and raising his hands.

"I'm sorry. I'll go to my office and give you space. I'm sure you're here to see how everything looks, so go on ahead."

"You don't need to go." *Please don't go.* "I wasn't saying that to you." She held her eyes closed. "I was lecturing myself and slipped up."

A soft laugh made her eyes snap open. "Sounded more like an argument than a lecture."

She nodded and couldn't help smiling a little in

return. "What my heart wants and what my head knows are two different things. But this can't affect our working together. You might hear me hissing orders to myself once in a while, but I'm sure that'll get better over time. Shall we go look at the room?"

"Oddly enough, I look forward to hearing you hiss like a teapot whenever you're around me." He opened the door. She moved past him when he continued. "And I want you around me as much as possible."

She stumbled and his hand closed on her arm. She should have pulled away. But she didn't.

"Quinn..."

She jumped when Courtney from the resort's restaurant came through a door on the far side of the room, pushing a metal serving cart piled high with dishes, napkins and trays of silverware. Courtney waved with a bright smile, and Julie and Quinn both waved back. Quinn lowered his head to speak into her ear.

"This isn't the place, but Julie...we need to talk. There has to be a way to fix this. Please..."

She gently pulled her arm free. "You need to say *no* to that internal voice of yours, like I just did. Our, um, chemistry isn't going to stop just because we've...stopped. So tell yourself no."

"Julie, please. I want you. Only you."

She wanted him, too. But she wasn't going to jump back into the same situation she'd just walked out of.

"I'm looking for someone who does more than *want* me, Quinn. I can't always be wondering if I'm enough."

The clatter of dishes and silverware reminded them they weren't alone. They dropped the conversation and walked through the room, which looked even better than she'd hoped. The flowers wouldn't arrive until morning, but the fluffy woodchucks were adorable sitting on the brightly decorated tables. It almost had a circus feel with all the colors.

She and Quinn carefully kept their conversation to business, discussing the schedule, the menu, the tournament. The serving tables were set up exactly where they should be. The sound system was ready for announcements and music. There was a small dance floor installed near the windows. It was wonderful. And Julie barely saw any of it.

I want you.

What was she supposed to *do* with that? How could she unhear it? And why did it give her the smallest, sharpest pinch of hope?

Chapter Eighteen

Quinn was glad to finally get home on Friday night. It had been an absolute madhouse at the golf club. It had also been a smashing success. The weather had been perfect, with bright sunny skies and a soft breeze. Quinn received loads of compliments on the condition of the golf course during the practice round. Everyone was excited for the big tournament tomorrow. Blake and Amanda had been beaming with happiness. And Julie had been her usual efficient self at the cocktail party—the Woman In Charge.

But he'd seen the furtive glances she'd sent his way. He had a feeling she knew at every moment exactly where he was in the room. To be fair, he was the same with her. She'd held his attention far more than any of the golfers had. He hadn't had a chance to talk to her more than a few fast words as she'd flown by.

Once everyone finally headed back to the resort, he made sure the night crew was all set locking up the clubhouse and went home, knowing he'd have to be up before dawn tomorrow for the tournament. He headed down to the dock bench to unwind in the light of the full moon before he tried to sleep.

"Dad?" Katie walked across the grass from the house and followed him out to the bench. "I saw your car pull in. How did things go today?"

"Hey, sweetheart." Quinn gave Katie a quick hug before they both sat. She handed him a beer, then held up her soda bottle so he'd know she was behaving. She'd be gone in two weeks, but he couldn't think about that tonight. His heart was being stretched too far this week as it was. "Everything was great. I just need to decompress…"

"Sorry I didn't come to the party tonight, but a couple of my friends wanted to go to The Chalet for pizza together before we head out to school."

"Trust me, you enjoyed that pizza a lot more than you would have enjoyed hanging out with a bunch of stodgy old people dressed like fools and drinking all night."

Her face scrunched up. "For sure."

He took a drink, then held up the bottle in a toast. "Thanks. I knew I raised you right."

"I don't know, Dad. Sometimes I wish I'd listened more to you *and* Mom."

Where was this mood coming from? "Hey, I'm proud of the amazing woman you've become, and your mom would be proud, too." He put his arm over her shoulders. "And if you ignored a few lessons along the way, well…that'll give me a chance to say *I told you so* someday."

She rested her head on his shoulder, ignoring his attempt at humor. Silence stretched out between them. He knew she had more to say, so he gave her time to put her thoughts together.

"Was Julie at the party?" She must have felt the way his body went still. "Dad, I'm really sorry I messed things up with you two."

"You did *not* mess things up." He kissed the top of her head. "It had nothing to do with you."

"It doesn't feel that way. It all went to hell when she heard us."

He stroked her hair. "That conversation exposed something that was going to come up eventually. She's hurt, and I'm—I'm a fool." For thinking he could have a second chance at love.

"Then go fix it." If only it was that easy.

"I tried. But forgetting your mom's birthday rattled me and—"

"Oh, no. Cassie was right."

"Right about what?"

"She and Amanda asked me to go to lunch with them the other day at work."

We'll handle Katie...

His jaw tightened. "Did they tell you this was your fault?"

"No! We just talked about me going to school and what it meant for you and then we talked about Mom..."

He knew Cassie and Amanda were trying to help, but he wasn't sure how he felt about this.

"What was it that Cassie was right about?"

Katie hesitated. "She said that you were afraid you couldn't love Julie because you already loved Mom. That freaked Julie out, and now you're both afraid."

"Sounds like you had quite a conversation. I'm surprised my ears weren't burning. Or Julie's. Since neither one of us was there." He wasn't thrilled that his daughter was hearing all this from anyone but him, but then again, he hadn't even tried to discuss it with her.

"It wasn't gossipy or mean, Dad. I promise. They were talking about love and how to know when it's real and I talked about how you and Mom were so in love and how you guys planned everything before she died. How she wanted to be remembered. How she..." Katie looked out over the water, which was the color of ink now. "How she wanted you to fall in love again."

"What?" Quinn straightened, anger rising. "Did they *tell* you that? Because it's not…"

"It *is* true, Dad." He objected, but she shut him down. "I know it's true because Mom *told* me." She put her hand on his. "Mom made me promise to help you find love again. Well…maybe not to *help*, but to not get in your way. She told me she wanted you to find someone. She wanted you to be happy." She paused to wipe her nose, sniffling. "And I blew it. I did exactly what Mom asked me not to do. I didn't help you find happiness, and then when you found it anyway, I got in your way."

Quinn's mind spun, stumbled and spun again. "Tell me what your mom told you. And when. How long before she…?"

"It was a month or so before she died." Katie told him about the quiet conversation she had with Anne the day the three of them had gone to the beach. He remembered the two of them sitting under the umbrella while he searched for the shells Anne loved. Through tears, Katie told him about the promise she thought she'd betrayed. First, by not encouraging him to date until right before she graduated, and then by interfering, even if unintentionally, with his relationship with Julie. He pulled her into his arms, overwhelmed with love and sorrow for what they'd both lost.

"Honey, what happened with Julie and me isn't

on you. She and I both have things from our pasts to work through."

"Yeah, Amanda and Cassie told me about Julie's childhood. Sounds like it was brutal. I mean, I lost my mom, but at least we were happy when she was alive. I have so many great memories." She sighed, her head against Quinn's chest. "But her mom was a drunk. She *hit* Julie. Like…a *lot*."

Quinn managed to hold in his surprise. Julie had always skirted around the details of how bad things were, and she'd never mentioned physical abuse. Just that her dad had left them and her mom was a mess from her addictions. Her great-grandmother had saved them.

"And her dad…"

"He left. I know."

"But the way he did it—promising to come back for her, then never doing it. She believed for the longest time. They said she used to wait at the window for him."

Quinn didn't react. That was another detail he hadn't known. No wonder Julie had withdrawn so sharply when she heard him talking about how much he'd loved Anne.

I can't always be wondering if I'm enough…

Being loved is more than Julie Brown has ever gotten in return from anyone she opened herself up to…

"Dad, I really like Julie. And she makes you

happy—happier than I've seen you in years. Don't lose her." She looked up at him with a crooked smile. "I think Mom would be really mad if you did."

Julie was up before dawn. She had to be at the resort before breakfast to make sure every last detail was ready for the big day. Staffing. Supplies. Food. Housekeeping. She wanted to be sure the ballroom was ready for tonight's gala.

She'd been invited to the start of the golf tournament, but she'd declined. The less she was anywhere near Quinn Walker today, the better. Instead, she made sure the nongolfers were happy, whether they'd opted for an excursion or if they were relaxing at the resort all day. The spa was fully booked with women wanting to look their best for the gala.

Julie left the spa and headed back down the grand staircase toward her office. She wondered if Quinn would come to the gala. She smiled to herself as she reached the lobby floor. If he did show up, he'd probably be in golf shorts and shirt. And he'd look good in them, too.

This was a new place they were in. They weren't mad at each other. The chemistry was still alive and well between them. But beyond that good news was a yawning chasm of uncertainty. Did he love her as much as he'd loved Anne? Did it *matter*? Maybe it shouldn't, but it did to Julie.

Her whole life, she'd craved security. She'd taken care of financial security, with a career, a degree and her own home. But when it came to love, she'd *never* felt secure, with the exception of her brother and grandmother. And in romance? She'd never come close. Until Quinn. But if *he* didn't know if he'd ever get over losing his wife, then how could *she* possibly trust him with her heart? It wasn't worth the risk, no matter how tempting. And she needed to find more to do to keep her from thinking about him. Because it was *very* tempting.

Lunchtime went smoothly, and she was hearing good reports from the golf tournament. It seemed that everyone was happy. She checked her watch—she needed to be in the suite where the "models" would be getting ready for the fashion show before five o'clock for hair and makeup. She reminded herself that despite her nerves, it was all for a good cause. She headed out to the pool area to make sure things were going smoothly there—plenty of towels and chairs available, with baskets of bottled water. She stood near the outdoor bar and kicked herself for being so darned good at her job. She couldn't find a single crisis—big or small—to deal with today, which meant she had more time to think. That just wouldn't do.

She headed down to the lakeshore. The lifeguard was watching over a handful of children splashing in the water. Their parents were watching too, from the comfort of the Adirondack chairs scattered near the small sand beach. Julie sighed. Nothing needed fixing here. But it was a pretty spot. Waves lapped at the shoreline, and she found herself walking away from the beach and along the waterfront. If staying busy wasn't going to work to keep Quinn off her mind, maybe a mindless stroll would do it.

She didn't realize how far she'd walked until she heard the familiar ping of a driver hitting a golf ball. She'd walked all the way to the golf course. *Thanks, universe.* Careful not to make any noise, she watched four men tee off and head down the fairway. Three of them had strong, clean swings, and the fourth was clearly a rookie. He was standing too straight, let his arms bend too much and lifted his head. His shot went wide right.

Julie huffed a laugh at herself. Look at her—a fancy golf critic now, thanks to Quinn's lessons. Another group approached the tee, and Julie figured she'd better get out of there before she distracted anyone. She turned, watching her footing on the rocks, and nearly walked right into Quinn's solid chest. Startled, she would have cried out if he hadn't put his fingers over her mouth.

"Shh!" He led her closer to the water, away from the golfers. "Sorry for startling you. What are you doing out here?"

"What do you think I'm doing? I'm taking a

walk." Her heart was still racing from the way he'd sneaked up on her.

"I thought maybe you were spying to see how things were going over here." His voice dropped. "Or maybe you were remembering what happened the first time we were in this spot."

She looked around, then groaned. It couldn't have been a coincidence that she ended up walking to the exact spot they'd first kissed.

Great way to avoid thinking about him, Julie.

"Aren't you supposed to be running a golf tournament?"

"Aren't you supposed to be running a resort?" Before she could answer, he surprised her again by resting his hands on her shoulders. "Let's forget about our territories, Jules. I'm *glad* you're here. We really need to talk."

"This isn't the time, Quinn. We're both busy—"

"And yet here we are, both standing in the same secluded spot by the water. I came down here because, tournament or not, I can't stop thinking about you. Why are you here?"

"I'm here because…" She gave a small shrug. "Same reason, I guess. Everything's going so well at the resort that there's nothing for me to do except think. Nothing has changed. I know what I need, and you can't give it."

"But what if I *can*?" He cupped her cheek with one hand, and she couldn't help leaning into it. His simple, tender touch was enough to weaken her resistance. To stall her protest. To rattle the bars around her heart. "Julie, I was up all night thinking about us. I *love* you. And, no, it's not the same way I loved Anne, but that doesn't make it *less*."

She went still, trying to put those words together in some logical order. He seemed excited, but he was confirming her worst fear.

"I understand you loved your wife, and I'm—I'm glad you did. I'm glad you still *do*. This isn't about me versus her. It's about me needing to be first in your heart *now*. And you've already admitted you don't know if—"

"I was an idiot when I said that." His voice was warm, but firm. "You've talked about what you deserve, and you're right. You *do* deserve to never have any reason to doubt my love." Beyond the thin line of trees, the second foursome left the tee, and another group was approaching. The world was going on around them, but in this little bubble, everything had stopped. The corner of Quinn's mouth lifted into a slanted grin. "While you were focused on what you *did* deserve, I was focused on what I *didn't*. I didn't think I deserved a second chance at love. I figured I'd had it once, and it would be selfish to want another. Then you came along and made me hope again. But I was so scared that I couldn't give you the love you deserved." He gave his head a quick shake. "Does that make any sense? I'm talking in circles here, probably because I didn't get any sleep."

She didn't want to surrender to hope without knowing where he was heading. "I'll admit I'm a little confused."

He laughed softly, glancing toward the golfers to make sure he hadn't distracted them. "I was, too. Look, what it comes down to is, I love you, babe. With my whole heart. You need to know you can rely on my love, and I promise you can. I'll work every day for the rest of my life to prove it. You can trust me. You can trust my love will be everything you need."

It sounded wonderful. It was exactly what she wanted. There was only one problem.

"You just told me that you'd never love me the way you loved your first wife."

"That's true." His smile grew. "Because you're not her. Don't you see? I kept putting Anne in the middle of us, and she doesn't belong there. I *did* love her. Our romance, our marriage—it was wonderful, and I don't want to dismiss a minute of it."

"Is this supposed to be making me feel better?" Julie stepped back, immediately regretting the loss of his touch. But she needed the space for clarity. "I don't want to sound like some ogre who doesn't want you to remember a wonderful marriage, but—"

"Let me finish," Quinn begged. "*Please*...hear me out. What I've finally realized is that it isn't an either-or situation. It's not a *choice* between loving Anne and loving you. I can do both." He grimaced. "That didn't sound right. I haven't had a chance to rehearse this."

Julie still had no idea what he was trying to tell her, but she had a feeling it was something—once he stopped stumbling over his words—that offered hope. *Real* hope. The kind of hope she was afraid to move toward, but that she didn't dare step any farther back from…just in case.

"You're not the kind to rehearse, Quinn. That's my thing, not yours." She felt the smile tugging at her mouth but tried to fight it off. "You're Mr. Spontaneous, remember?"

They heard someone hitting a drive behind them, and the murmur of approving voices. Their entire conversation so far had been in the hushed voices of golf announcers on television. Quinn rubbed his neck and looked at the lake.

"Well, I'm living up to that title right now—walking off the golf course, jumping into the most important conversation of my life without any planning. I'm beginning to think a little self-control on my part might be a good thing." His laughter was soft and affectionate. "And seriously—what *was* I saying? Seeing your beautiful smile just now wiped my mind blank."

"You were saying something about not making a choice."

"Exactly!" He cringed at the sudden volume. His voice grew quiet, his expression intense. "I didn't think I deserved another chance to fall in love. I couldn't get past the thought that it wouldn't be fair to my memories of Anne. When Katie got so upset about forgetting her mom's birthday, I felt like I was doing exactly what I was so afraid of. I was forgetting Anne." He paused. "And here I am, putting her right in the middle of us again. What I'm trying to say is two things can be true at the same time—I loved my first wife. And I'll love my second one, if she'll have me."

Julie's eyes went wide. Did she hear what she thought she heard?

"Did you just *propose* to me?" She wasn't using her golf-announcer voice anymore. "What are you thinking? We're not even together—"

"But we *could* be." He took her by her shoulders. "Julie, I'm not asking you to marry me today. I'm not even asking you to *answer* me today. But yes, I'm telling you that I want you to be my wife. And, no, I won't love you the same as I loved Anne. And you wouldn't want me to, because you're not her. I loved Anne for lots of reasons. I loved her sweetness, her easygoing attitude and the way she supported my career. I loved the way she snorted when she laughed. I loved her for having my daughter and loving Katie so damn much."

He pulled her closer, and she was too stunned to

resist. This was no ordinary marriage proposal. "But I love *you*, Julie Brown, for your strength and, yes, your take-charge attitude. I love you because you hate being spontaneous, but you're willing to try. I love you for being a bridesmaid fourteen times, even when it hurt. I love you for the way you've supported Katie since the day you met her." His arms slid around her, and she found herself clutching at his shirt for balance as his words swirled around her like a cyclone.

"I love how driven you are—you want to be good at everything you do. Getting a bachelor's degree wasn't enough for you, so you're going after your master's. I love the way you charge into solving problems. I love the way you fight for what you believe is right, even when you're fighting *me* to do it. I love the way you're so fiercely loyal to your friends, and I especially love how fiercely loyal they are to you. Your found family sees the same amazing woman that I do. And, baby…" Quinn pulled her close enough to kiss her temple, while his hands slid down to cup her behind. She felt a fire rekindling inside of her. "I love the way you kiss me. I love the way you slowly pull off your clothes when you know I'm watching, like my own private striptease. I love the way you shudder every time my fingers move across your skin, like you can't wait to see what happens next. I love the way you breathe when we're making love, in those little gasps and sighs that shoot straight through me. I love—"

"Okay," she whispered against his neck. She wasn't sure which of them was trembling more. "I get the message. But…" Her voice trailed off. She had no idea what her objection was.

Quinn's hand rose to brush the back of her head, and he smoothed her hair as if to calm her. Somehow he knew exactly what she needed. She stood there, head on his chest, letting her feelings wash over her in waves. Her entire life she'd considered herself unworthy of love, thanks to her childhood. But Quinn's list of reasons why he *did* love her rang so true that it was impossible to dismiss them.

His fingers moved to lift her chin, giving him easier access to kiss her. His lips were tentative at first, but she rose up on her toes to kiss him back, and he understood. *Kiss me harder.* Her hands ran through his hair, knocking his golf cap to the ground. Their heads turned and the kiss ignited.

Her phone began ringing in her pocket, and she jumped and bumped her head on Quinn's nose. He was rubbing it when his phone began to ring, too. They both stepped back and said *hello* at the same time.

"Julie?" It was Blake. His voice was more abrupt than usual. "What's going on at the resort?"

Her heart dropped. "Um, I don't know… I mean… why?" She started imagining all the terrible things that could have happened in her absence.

Next to her, Quinn sounded just as concerned on his call.

"What do you mean, the final green is a *mess*? Of course, I'm on the golf course, Shane. Where else would I be?"

They stared at each other, their intimacy broken by the intrusion of their jobs. Then Quinn looked up the hill over her shoulder and muttered a sharp curse, ending his phone call. She heard laughter from the tee box, and turned, phone still to her ear. The four men on the tee were Blake, Shane, Nick and the police chief, Dan Adams. They were looking at Quinn and Julie, nudging each other and laughing.

Still on the phone, Blake continued. "As your employer, I'm worried it might be hard for the two of you to run the most important event of the year when you're playing Romeo and Juliet by the waterfront instead of, you know…running things." He chuckled. "As your *friend*…well done, you two. I'm glad you figured things out." He ended the call, but raised his wrist as they watched and tapped his watch. They both got the point—they really did have jobs to get to. Quinn led Julie to the shadow of a large oak tree, out of sight from the amused golfers.

She reached up and rested her hand on his cheek. "I have to go."

He let out a sigh. "It's going to be a long day for us both. I want to be sure you know that I mean every word I said, though. You are *everything* to me. Please, tell me you're ready to take the leap and love me back."

Her smile faltered, but held. "You know I love you. You've given me a *lot* to think about. Including that kinda-sorta-maybe marriage proposal you slipped in there. But our boss is watching, and we *do* have jobs to think about. I know you don't want to hear it, but this will have to wait until after the tournament, which is where *you* should be, and to-night's gala, which is what *I* need to get ready for."

Had this just been another moment of impul-siveness from Mr. Spontaneous? Or was it really a chance at forever?

Quinn's expression made it clear he was frus-trated at the delay, but also resigned to it. "After the gala then. Katie and I will be there for the dinner and fashion show, but I know you'll be crazy-busy all night. Meet me right here when you're done. I'll wait as long as it takes." He brushed back a strand of hair that had blown across her face. "But, Julie... only meet me if you're ready for us to be together. For real, this time. No more practicing."

She nodded, brushing a kiss against his lips be-fore answering.

"If I'm here, it will be because I'm ready."

Chapter Nineteen

Quinn watched Julie walk toward him along the shoreline that night. With the black dress and her dark hair, she vanished whenever she walked through a shadow near the trees, then would appear again like the shadow had come to life in the moonlight. The diagonal slash of crystals shimmered the same way the tips of the waves did out on the water.

The dress had shimmered under the ballroom lights, too. He and Katie had gone to the gala and cheered Julie on together. But he'd kept his distance. She wasn't there as a guest—she was working. She'd been on the go all evening, checking the kitchen, making sure everyone found their tables and were served promptly. Her quick twirl in the fashion show was probably the only moment she hadn't been actively managing the room.

But Quinn hadn't been able to resist brushing against her near the bar. Her hair was slicked back into a tight twist, with one long curling tendril touching her neck behind her ear. The twist was held in place with a bejeweled clip that matched the crystals on her dress.

"Something about that dress looks familiar," he'd murmured at her side. Julie had turned and smiled.

"You recognize the pink, eh? Luis did a great job."

They'd chatted for a moment, talking about the fashion show and how successful the fundraising efforts had been—the foundation's best event ever. Her eyes seemed clear of the caution that had clouded them this past week. He hoped that was a good sign. He asked if he'd see her later, and she'd coyly patted his cheek.

"I guess you'll have to wait and see."

She walked up to him now, her smile wide and brighter than any gems. "Walking this shoreline in these heels is an adventure." She laughed, then met his eyes. "What?"

"You don't look real right now. I can't decide if you're a wood nymph or a water sprite, with all that black satin and sparkle."

"Well, let's see…" She stepped into his open arms and kissed him, her lips soft and warm against his. He held her tight and gladly returned the kiss, groaning when she pulled her head back. "So...did that feel real to you?"

"Hmm. Let's try it again to be sure." His hands slid up to cup her face and he kissed her again. Deeper. Longer. And far more grateful than he'd ever felt. His lips brushed her cheek and he spoke against her skin. "Feels real to me. I love you so damn much."

She pulled back and stared into his eyes. "I believe you."

Those three words meant everything to him. It was a higher hurdle than her loving him. He knew she loved him. But to win her *trust*? That meant she was truly his. And he'd never give her another chance to doubt his love again. She snuggled into his arms, resting her head on his shoulder.

"Our friends will be expecting us at the after-party up at Halcyon."

"Let them wait. I'm not ready to share you right now. I just want to stand here and hold you."

"You won't hear any complaints from me." She touched a kiss to the bottom of his neck, sending a surge of adrenaline through his body. "But once the mosquitoes find us, we won't be able to stay here very long. You know that, right?"

He chuckled. "Good point. Are you going to change?" The after-party was generally a casual affair.

Julie shrugged. "I'd like to, but I might need some help getting out of this dress."

His arms tightened around her. "I think I know someone who can assist with that."

"I was hoping you would." She looked up at him through long lashes. "You're going to be handy to have around."

"I'm glad you think so, 'cause I'm not planning on going anywhere."

"Oh, no...*fore*!" Julie shouted down the fairway as Quinn laughed behind her. Her drive had gone sharply to the right, onto the neighboring fairway.

"You're safe—there aren't any golfers ahead of us this morning."

"Thank God." She gave him a saucy pose, leaning on her club like a dancer with a cane. She was beginning to enjoy their golf rounds. Or maybe it was just being with him she enjoyed so much. "But did you see how far it went?"

Quinn laughed. "It went in the wrong direction, but it definitely went far. For you."

Julie stuck her tongue out at him, then dropped her club into her bag on the cart so they could go to Quinn's ball, which had gone much farther than hers, *and* managed to stay on the correct fairway. It was a gorgeous early September morning. The sky was showing hints of autumn with its brilliant blue color. There was a brisk breeze blowing, and the lake was choppy, with bright white caps on the waves. She grabbed a light jacket from the back of the cart as Quinn hit his ball onto the green.

"Are you cold? We don't have to do eighteen holes today."

"Are you kidding? We're in a big tournament next week, and I'm going to have to be able to golf eighteen holes for that, so get in the cart and drive, buster!"

He tried not to laugh at her but failed. "I know it's your *first* tournament, but it is not a *big* tournament. It's just a fun competition to benefit the high school sports programs. And you won't be playing eighteen holes on your own—it's a captain-and-crew game, so you're part of a team of four. We play the best ball each hole…" He stopped the cart next to her ball, sitting in the wrong fairway. "And that's probably not going to be yours all that often."

"Oh, gee, thanks, coach. Have you ever considered that my lousy game reflects more on you than me?" She started to get out of the cart, then stopped. She looked back at Quinn, tanned and relaxed. His arm rested on the back of the seat, and one eyebrow rose in question.

"What is it?" She sat back, sliding over so he could put his arm around her. His forehead creased. "Are you tired? Too cold? We really can quit, you know."

She shook her head. "I'm not quitting. I just…"

She rested her hand on his chest, and his eyes went dark with desire. She loved that all it took was a touch. "Look at us. A few months ago we were fighting in Blake's office. And now…we're *golfing* together. We're in love and practically living together."

Now that Katie was in Tallahassee—and with her enthusiastic blessing—Julie and Fluff had pretty much moved into the lake house. They hadn't decided what to do with Julie's place—sell it or keep it as a rental property. "Sometimes it…overwhelms me. But it all feels so *right*, you know? Unexpected, but meant to be. How lucky are we?"

Quinn put two fingers under her chin and lowered his head to stare straight into her eyes. "I tried to tell you to embrace the unexpected. I never thought I'd fall in love again, yet here we are. Life is funny sometimes."

She paused, trying to put her thoughts into words. "Sometimes I feel so much happiness with you that I don't know what to do with it all. Right now I want to go twirling around across the fairway with pure joy, and that is *not* me at all. At least it didn't used to be."

A revelation hit her, and she sat up straight. She thought of all those bridesmaid dresses. More than half were gone now, thanks to the charity show. "Oh, my God, I'm just like the bridesmaid dresses!"

Quinn squinted at her. "I have no idea what that means."

"I'm not the person I used to be. I'm, well…*recycled* doesn't sound right, but maybe *transformed*?"

"You're saying we make each other better by being together?"

"I think so, yes."

He pulled her back to his side and kissed her long and slow.

"Well, that's good. Especially since we're going to be together for the rest of our lives." His eyes were shining with emotion. "I love you, Julie Brown."

She closed her eyes briefly, as if that would help her capture her joy at those words. And at her ability to *believe* them. She trusted the man. And she trusted his love.

"I love you, too, Quinn Walker. And I always will."

* * * * *

For more opposites attract romances,
try these great romances:

A Fortune in the Family
By Kathy Douglass

Reluctant Roommates
By Tara Taylor Quinn

Captivated by the Cowgirl
By Brenda Harlen

Available now wherever
Harlequin Special Edition books and ebooks
are sold!

WE HOPE YOU ENJOYED
THIS BOOK FROM

⬡ HARLEQUIN
SPECIAL
EDITION

Believe in love. Overcome obstacles. Find happiness.

Relate to finding comfort and strength in the
support of loved ones and enjoy the journey
no matter what life throws your way.

6 NEW BOOKS AVAILABLE EVERY MONTH!

#2911 FINDING FORTUNE'S SECRET
The Fortunes of Texas: The Wedding Gift • by Allison Leigh

Stefan Mendoza has found Justine Maloney in Texas nearly a year after their whirlwind Miami romance. Now that he's learned he's a father, he wants to "do the right thing." But for Justine, marriage without love is a deal breaker. And simmering below the surface is a family secret that could change everything for them both—forever...

#2912 BLOOM WHERE YOU'RE PLANTED
The Friendship Chronicles • by Darby Baham

Jennifer Pritchett feels increasingly left behind as her friends move on to the next steps in their lives. As she goes to therapy to figure out how to bloom in her own right, her boyfriend, Nick Carrington, finds himself being the one left behind. Can they each get what they need out of this relationship? Or will the flowers shrivel up before they do?

#2913 THE TRIPLETS' SECRET WISH
Lockharts Lost & Found • by Cathy Gillen Thacker

Emma Lockhart and Tom Reid were each other's one true love—until their dueling ambitions drove them apart. Now Emma has an opportunity that could bring the success she craves. When Tom offers his assistance in exchange for her help with his triplets, Emma can't resist the cowboy's pull on her heart. Maybe her real success lies in taking a chance on happily-ever-after...

#2914 A STARLIGHT SUMMER
Welcome to Starlight • by Michelle Major

When eight-year-old Anna Johnson asked Ella Samuelson for help in fixing up her father with a new wife, Ella only agreed because she knew the child and her father had been through the wringer. Too bad she found herself drawn to the handsome and kind single dad!

#2915 THE LITTLE MATCHMAKER
Top Dog Dude Ranch • by Catherine Mann

Working at the Top Dog Dude Ranch is ideal for contractor Micah Fuller as he learns to parent his newly adopted nephew. But school librarian Susanna Levine's insistence that young Benji needs help reading has Micah overwhelmed. Hiring Susanna as Benji's tutor seems perfect...until Benji starts matchmaking. Micah would give his nephew anything, but getting himself a wife? A feat considering Susanna is adamant about keeping their relationship strictly business.

#2916 LOVE OFF THE LEASH
Furever Yours • by Tara Taylor Quinn

When Pets for Vets volunteer pilot Greg Martin's plane goes down after transporting a dog, coordinator Wendy Alvarez is filled with guilt. She knows a service dog will help, but Greg's just too stubborn. If Wendy can get him to "foster" Jedi, she's certain his life will be forever altered. She just never expected hers to change, as well.

YOU CAN FIND MORE INFORMATION ON UPCOMING HARLEQUIN TITLES, FREE EXCERPTS AND MORE AT HARLEQUIN.COM.

HSECNM0422

"You still don't belong here." Mariella crossed her arms
over her chest, and Alex commanded himself not to notice
her body, perfect as it was.

"That makes two of us, and yet here we are."

"I was here first," she muttered. He'd heard the argument
before, but it didn't sway him.

"You're not running me off, Mariella. I needed a fresh
start, and this is the place I've picked for my home."

"My plan was to leave the past behind me. You are a
physical reminder of so many mistakes I've made."

"I can't say that upsets me too much," he lied. It didn't
make sense, but he hated that he made her so uncomfortable.
Hated even more that sometimes he'd purposely drive by

her shop to get a glimpse of her through the picture window. Talk about a glutton for punishment.

She let out a low growl. "You are an infuriating man. Stubborn and callous. I don't even know if you have a heart."

"Funny." He kept his voice steady even as memories flooded him, making his head pound. "That's the rationale Amber gave me for why she cheated with your fiancé. My lack of emotions pushed her into his arms. What was his excuse?"

She looked out at the street for nearly a minute, and Alex wondered if she was even going to answer. He followed her gaze to the park across the street, situated in the center of the town. There were kids at the playground and several families walking dogs on the path that circled the perimeter. Magnolia was the perfect place to raise a family.

If a person had the heart to be that kind of a man—the type who married the woman he loved and set out to be a good husband and father. Alex wasn't cut out for a family, but he liked it in the small coastal town just the same.

"I was too committed to my job," she said suddenly and so quietly he almost missed it.

"Ironic since it was your job that introduced him to Amber."

"Yeah." She made a face. "This is what I'm talking about, Alex. A past I don't want to revisit."

"Then stay away from me, Mariella," he advised. "Because I'm not going anywhere."

"Then maybe I will," she said and walked away.

Don't miss
Wedding Season *by Michelle Major,*
available May 2022 wherever
HQN books and ebooks are sold.

HQNBooks.com

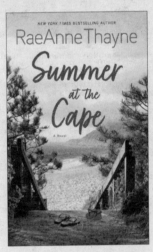